ON THE HOOK

Also by

FRANCISCO X. STORK

Illegal

Disappeared

The Memory of Light

Irises

The Last Summer of the Death Warriors

Marcelo in the Real World

ON THE HOOK

FRANCISCO X. STORK

SCHOLASTIC PRESS
NEW YORK

11/21

All rights reserved. Published by Scholastic Press, an imprint of Scholastic Inc., *Publishers since 1920*. SCHOLASTIC, SCHOLASTIC PRESS, and associated logos are trademarks and/or registered trademarks of Scholastic Inc.

The publisher does not have any control over and does not assume any responsibility for author or third-party websites or their content.

Library of Congress Cataloging-in-Publication Data available

ISBN 978-1-338-69215-0

1 2021

Printed in the U.S.A.   23

First edition, May 2021

Book design by Christopher Stengel

FOR WILLEM XAVIER
KLOOSTERBOER

CHAPTER 1

Hector could tell that Azi wanted to discuss something. He started to turn right on Alameda Avenue, but Azi walked in the direction of the residential neighborhood and the irrigation ditch. It was the longer route to the Kennedy Brothers Apartments, otherwise known as the projects, but it was quieter, better for talking. They had just come out of a chess team meeting where Mr. Lozano announced that next year's captain would be determined by a competition among the team's members. Azi had looked meaningfully in Hector's direction. Now Hector waited for her to say what he knew was coming.

"Well?" Azi asked when they had left the noise of traffic behind them.

"Well what?" Hector pretended ignorance.

"You're trying out for captain, right?"

"I don't know. I'm not sure I'm captain material." It was good to say that, even if it wasn't true. "Besides, it's kind of an unwritten rule that the captain of the chess team should be a senior."

"Where? Where is it unwritten?"

They both laughed.

Azi went on. "And don't say you're not good enough to be captain. I'm Iranian, remember? In Iran it is bad manners to show off, so everyone goes around pretending to be humble. You're the best player in the team and you know it. The purpose of having a competition instead of an election is to have the captain be the best player."

"Mendoza is pretty good, and he really, really wants to be captain. And he's a junior and we're lowly sophomores."

"Oh, please!" Azi threw her hands up in the air as if asking heaven for help. "Has he beaten you?"

"Yes . . . once." Hector smiled. Mendoza was a top-caliber player, but he was better. The loss to him the year before, just after Hector joined the chess team, was the result of a bonehead move on Hector's part and not because of any kind of brilliant move by Mendoza. When you played and studied the strategies of chess as much as Hector did, you knew with certainty when your game was at a higher level than someone else's. Still, Hector liked Mendoza, and being the captain of the Ysleta High Chess Team would mean a lot to him.

They were approaching the house where a large brown dog always snarled at them through the backyard's gate.

They simultaneously walked to the opposite sidewalk. When they were far away from the dog, Azi said, her tone suddenly serious, "Hector, you need to keep in mind two things: First, the team should have the best player as captain. The captain is a teacher to the other players. Having the best player as the captain is what is best for the team."

"Mmm." Hector momentarily imagined standing in front of the whole team, explaining the individual moves of the 1972 world championship match between Bobby Fischer and Boris Spassky. Hector stopped to pick up a baseball that had rolled to the sidewalk. He tossed it back to the front lawn of the house near a bat and child's glove. "You know," he said, "now that I think of it, *you* should be captain. You're a better player than Mendoza and you are very good at giving instructions." Hector tried to keep himself from smiling but was unable.

"Did you just insult me?" Azi asked.

"I meant that you give really good advice. It was a compliment."

"Yeah, sure. For your information, I would enter the competition for captain if I honestly thought I was the best player."

"Who says you're not?"

"Have I ever won a single match against you?"

"No," Hector said, "but that's only because I spend more time studying chess than you. You have your science projects and math club and college-level courses. Let's just say that if you put some effort into it, you could beat me . . . in a year . . . or two."

Azi laughed. Hector liked it when she laughed. Azi, who was always so dignified and proper in school, felt comfortable enough to laugh and joke with him.

"I *am* smarter than you in most ways." Azi looked at Hector, waited for him to protest, and then continued. "But not when it comes to chess. Chess comes natural to you. You have an instinct for making the right moves at the right time. You're a chess . . ."

"Yes? Go on—I think you're actually going to say something nice."

Besides making Azi laugh, Hector enjoyed the rare occasions when he made her blush.

"No, I'm not going to say the word you think I was going to say. It will go to your empty head."

They walked on in silence. Sometimes he and Azi would walk together like that, each lost in their own thoughts. They had been walking back to the projects together since their freshman year when they'd found out, after the first meeting of the chess team, that they lived a block away from each other. During their first walk, they'd discovered they had something else in common besides the love of chess: Both of them had lost their father in the past year.

Thinking about that conversation, and thinking about his

father, reminded Hector now of the house they lived in before his father had died. It was a four-bedroom cream-colored ranch with flower beds leading up to the front door and a chili pepper garden that his father had cared for meticulously in the backyard. Hector quickly brushed the memory away and asked, "You said there were two things I needed to keep in mind. One was that the captain of the chess team should be the best player. What was the other?"

"The other," Azi said without missing a beat, "is that you need to stick to your plan for the future just like I need to stick to mine."

"The one where you get a scholarship to a great college and then to a great medical school and then become a great brain surgeon."

"Neurosurgeon. That's my plan. And yours?"

"I become a chess grandmaster before my eighteenth birthday and go on to win the world championship and get super rich doing commercials for luxury cars," Hector said, rolling his eyes.

"Hector, be serious for a moment."

"Okay. What I really want is to get me and my family out of the stupid, miserable housing projects where we live."

Azi nodded and waited for Hector to calm down. Then she said softly, soothingly, "And to do that you need to get a scholar-ship so you can go to college and become the engineer you want to be. Being the captain of the Ysleta High School Chess Team is something that will help you get that scholarship."

They reached the end of the street and then climbed up the embankment to the top of the ditch. The ditch was dry now, but Hector knew that once a week water flowed through it to irrigate the one or two cotton fields that had survived the area's development. The same ditch crossed the neighborhood where Hector and his family used to live. His father had liked to come to the ditch on Sunday afternoons and wade his feet into the murky flow. Hector's older brother, Filiberto— or Fili, as everyone called him—had no problem jumping in, but Hector preferred to sit on the banks. He had seen snakes slither in and out of the ditch, and once, Fili had pulled a dead cat from the rushing current.

On the side of the ditch where they walked, there was a dirt road wide enough for a car to travel, plus a few places where kids could drive up or down the slopes of the embankment with their cars. The beer cans, cheap wine bottles, and used condoms strewn around were a reminder to Hector that they were approaching the housing projects.

"Just promise me you'll think about it," Azi said.

"I promise," Hector said, distracted by a blue car parked up ahead on the dirt road. The sound of music and laughter reached them.

"We better turn around," Hector said.

Azi shaded her eyes with her hand and peered. "It's just some kids drinking."

"It's a blue Impala," Hector said.

"So?"

"It's Chavo's car."

Chavo, their local drug dealer, lived with his younger brother, Joey, in the building next to Hector's. Joey was sixteen, just like Hector. They were even in the same social studies class except that Joey rarely showed up—and when he did, he picked a desk in the back of the class and slept. Hector had always tried to stay under Chavo and Joey's radar, but something had changed in the past two weeks. Recently, there had been enough hostile stares and belligerent gestures by both Chavo and Joey to make Hector believe that he had been noticed and even singled out. Or it could be that his fear of those two was making him see what wasn't there.

"Do you really want to go all the way back to Alameda?" Azi said. "They're inside the car. We'll go down and walk on the path beside the ditch. They won't see us."

They climbed down the ditch, Azi leading the way. It was embarrassing to have Azi see him act like a scared rabbit. But then again Azi knew that it made good sense to stay as far away as possible from Chavo and his friends.

"I need . . ." Azi started to speak, but Hector raised his

finger to his lips. She tried again, this time whispering. "I need to ask you a favor."

"What?"

"Will you teach me to play basketball? In gym class, I'm the only player who's never made a basket. I'm terrible. No one ever passes the ball to me. We can go to the playground in front of your apartment building."

"No, not there." Hector nodded in the direction of the blue car. "Chavo and his brother hang out there. We can practice after school at the courts there. I'll borrow Aurora's basketball."

"When?"

Hector touched his lips with his finger. "Tomorrow morning, first thing. I'll call you."

"But you work on Saturdays."

"Not tomorrow. Frank changed my shift to this evening."

The back door of the blue car opened, and out came Joey. Hector and Azi stopped and watched him step to the front of the car and begin to urinate, a cigarette hanging from his left hand. Hector tried to pull Azi behind a bush, but Azi wouldn't budge.

Joey was zipping up his pants when his eyes landed on Hector and Azi. He jerked his head back with surprise, and then, looking directly at Azi, his face broke into an ugly, leering grin.

"You like what you saw?" he taunted.

"You're disgusting," Azi said, looking away from him and heading off.

Joey's grin disappeared, and when he next spoke, it was to Hector. "That hynita's too hot for a pendejo like you." A woman laughed from inside the car and Joey went back in. Just before he closed the door to the car, Joey said to Hector, "I'll be looking for you. Soon."

Hector didn't reply. Instead he caught up to Azi, who was now climbing to the top of the ditch again.

"Big jerk," she muttered as she brushed dust from her skirt. Then, as if the whole interaction hadn't happened, she resumed their conversation from before. "Maybe Aurora can come to our basketball lessons. She's on the eighth-grade basketball team, isn't she?"

Hector was still thinking about Joey's words. Were they a threat? They had to be a threat. So he hadn't been imagining things after all. Joey was focused on him.

But why?

"Hector, where did you go? You're not going to let that guy get to you. He's not worth thinking about."

"Nothing fazes you, does it?"

"Guys like that?" Azi jerked her head toward the blue car behind them. "Pssh. I'm not going to let them interfere with my life."

"Yeah, well. Don't underestimate guys like that. I see what they do from the window of my room. Joey is plain nasty. Just ask some of the kids at school he's beaten up. And Chavo is worse. Word is, he once killed a junkie who stole from him." Hector shook his head. "I miss being able to walk outside after dark. I miss sleeping through the night without waking up to loud music or people shouting obscenities."

"It's not perfect, but it's a lot better than where my family came from."

"You still need to be careful" was all that Hector could think of saying.

"You sound like my mother." Azi laughed.

Then she started running, her backpack bouncing heavily on her back. Hector watched for a few seconds and then took off after her.

CHAPTER 2

Hector walked Azi to her apartment and then ran home. There was a note on the kitchen table from Aurora:

Mami and me went to the Hijas de Guadalupe meeting at church. (I was forced to go!!!!) Mami says to make sure you eat before you head to work. There's a plate for you to microwave in the fridge.

Hector dropped the backpack on his bed and looked out of his window in the direction of Joey's apartment. The blue Impala was not back yet. That was good. Hector did not want to run into Joey again on his way to work. He decided to skip his mother's dinner and eat something from the cooked-food department of the Piggly Wiggly.

It was still light at seven when Hector walked to the back of the grocery store. Besides stacking and pricing, one of Hector's jobs was folding cardboard boxes and tossing them in the recycling bin. It was an easy job that allowed him to think about other things. That evening he was thinking about his brother, Fili. There was something different about him lately. He was coming home earlier than usual, and he did not reek of alcohol when he tumbled into bed.

Could it be that Fili was finally pulling out of the depression he had fallen into after Papá died?

Hector froze when he heard the roar from a car behind him. He turned quickly, but there was no blue Impala. It was just a delivery van in need of a new muffler. The whole thing with Joey had him rattled. *I'll be looking for you*? It seemed like a very specific thing to say. Specific words specifically directed at him. Hector remembered how Chavo had tossed a beer can in the back of Fili's truck the week before. It wasn't just a careless toss; there was anger in the way he threw the can. Hector later went out and picked up the can before Fili could see it. His brother was very protective of his truck, and if he'd seen the can, he'd have known it was Chavo and his friends who'd tossed it there. Fili was not afraid of anyone. He'd go up to Chavo and say a few choice words to him, or worse.

Hector heard footsteps behind him. A tremor ran through him. He knew, even before he turned around, that the footsteps were Joey's.

Maybe Joey needed a few empty boxes for the drug business. Frank, Hector's boss, had a rule that all empty box requests had to go through him, but Hector decided, right then and there, that if Joey wanted boxes, he could take as many as he wanted.

Hector scanned the loading docks for another Piggly Wiggly employee, but there was no one. The recycling containers were in a far corner of the lot, where the trucks could have enough room to back in and pull out. No one driving by on the street would see the containers. Hector reminded himself that the word in the projects was that Chavo could be violent for no reason, but there were no such rumors about Joey.

Joey had gotten into fights at school with kids who had disrespected him somehow. And what had Hector ever done or said to Joey? Nothing. There was no reason to be afraid. Except, Hector thought as he turned around, for the cold look on Joey's face, and the slow, purposeful way he was walking, like he meant to kill.

"What's up?" Hector said, trying to sound casual. Joey moved in closer than was needed for a normal conversation. Hector hugged an empty box of baby food against his chest.

"You think you the big mierda?" Joey asked. Joey's tone was different than when he'd called Hector a pendejo earlier. There was less insult in his voice. It was as if Joey had casually asked Hector for the time. There was a slight slur to his words, and Hector thought maybe Joey was drunk. He looked for other signs of inebriation, signs Hector was familiar with, but he didn't see any.

"I'm asking you. You think you the big mierda?"

The question jolted Hector. He had assumed from Joey's round, shaved head and tattooed neck that the kid was completely checked out. So why would Joey ask that? Had he heard about how he was the best chess player at school?

Realizing he owed Joey a response, Hector said hastily, "What? No. I don't think that. What are you talking about?"

Joey slapped the box from Hector's hands. Hector stepped back and tripped on the boxes he had yet to fold. Joey grabbed Hector's T-shirt and lifted him off his toes with the same ease with which Hector had been picking up empty boxes. Joey's face was so close to him that he could smell cinnamon on his breath.

"Look at me!" Joey ordered.

Hector forced himself to stare into Joey's eyes. The dark circles floated as if unhinged, but when they finally came to rest, Hector saw hatred there. Not the kind that blazed up with momentary anger but one that had been smoldering for a long time. But why? What had he ever done to Joey? This was not making any sense.

Hector stuck his right hand in his pocket to keep it from trembling. "What do you want?" he asked. He had to look away from Joey's steady stare.

Joey jerked Hector's hand out of the pocket. Then, pinning

Hector against the dumpster, he dug into Hector's pocket and pulled out a box cutter. He slid the small blade out and held it in front of Hector's face. "You gonna use this?"

Hector shook his head. "Let me go," he said weakly. What was it that Fili had once said to him about not showing fear? But it was useless to pretend he wasn't afraid or to try to manufacture courage he knew he didn't have.

Joey moved the blade in front of Hector's eyes as if trying to hypnotize him. "You and your pinche brother are nothing but pieces of stinking cagada."

"Okay."

"You're a coward."

"Okay."

"Okay? You're a coward?"

"I guess so."

"Say it."

"I'm . . . a coward."

"That chavita you were walking with earlier—what's her name?"

Hector shook his head.

Joey put his hands around Hector's neck, softly at first, and then he began to squeeze.

"What's her name?"

"Azarakhsh Pourmohammadi," Hector said between gasps.

"What?"

"It's . . . her . . . name." Hector tried to pull Joey's arm away.

"Where's she from? Las Cruces?" Joey roared with laughter. There was a joke in there somewhere, but only Joey knew where.

Hector stood on his toes to relieve the pressure, but Joey's grip gradually increased until all air coming into Hector's lungs was cut off. Then, just as Hector was about to lose consciousness, Joey let him go. Hector sank to his knees, coughing and gagging. As soon as he could breathe, Joey pulled Hector's hair until Hector was on his feet again.

"Listen to me, culero." Joey grabbed Hector's face and held it until Hector's eyes were focused. "I'm gonna kill you."

"Please! No!"

"Cállate. I'm talking. I'm gonna do it. I'm gonna slice you up. Not now. Soon. I want you to think about it. Every pinche minute of your pinche vida you be thinking about it. Be waiting for it. And this is so you don't forget you're a gusano. A mierda, a cobarde." Joey stuck his forearm in Hector's neck and pushed his head hard against the recycling container. He lifted Hector's T-shirt and slowly carved a C in the left side of Hector's chest, above his heart. It was a thin cut, only the depth of the skin, and Hector was surprised when it did not hurt at first. Then there was a slight burning sensation that gradually increased until his whole body ached. Hector tightened his jaw to prevent himself from crying out. He felt the saltiness of tears fill his eyes.

"Why?" It was all he could think of saying.

"I own you, puto," Joey said, a few inches from Hector's face. "From now on you're mine. You be saying, *When will he come to get me?* You be asking, *Where?* Maybe after school. Or when you're walking home with your putita. Maybe tomorrow. Maybe next year. Thing is, you know I'm coming. You're dead already."

Only then did Joey step back and remove his arm from Hector's neck. He looked at Hector's chest one more time as if to admire his handiwork, then gently pulled down Hector's T-shirt. Hector looked down, saw the red spread through the white cotton. Joey stuck the box cutter in Hector's pocket and said, offhand, "Oh, you rat to anyone about this and something bad will happen to your carnalita. What's her name, Aurora? I know where you live, cabrón."

Hector sank to the ground and watched Joey walk slowly away. After a while, when he was sure Joey was gone, he sat up. He tore a piece of cardboard from a box and pressed it against the cut in his chest. The bleeding had slowed to a trickle. The employee restroom was near the back entrance to the store. He would put some paper towels on the cut and then grab one of the yellow T-shirts that the store asked the cashiers to wear.

His whole body throbbed with pain, but only some of it came from the cut. What hurt the most was the knowledge that he had not fought back. Not nearly enough. He had given Azi's full name when Joey had asked for it. He'd stood there and taken what Joey gave him. Then, when it was all over, he'd cried. He'd been paralyzed by fear, and the fear was still in him, much stronger than before.

He was a coward, and the proof of it was branded on his chest.

CHAPTER 3

Hector bought gauze pads, medical tape, and anti-biotic cream at the store and patched his wound in the employee bathroom before heading home. Once there, he hid behind parked cars until he saw the light in his mother's bedroom window go off. He waited another fifteen minutes before entering the apartment. He walked straight to the bathroom, showered, changed bandages, and went to bed. The bleeding had stopped, but now there was a raw, burning sensation in his chest. It almost felt good to have a physical reminder of the shame he felt inside. The memory of his father came to him. His father had come home from the hospital knowing that he had maybe one or two months left of life before the lung cancer killed him.

A few days before his father died, Hector had asked him, "Are you afraid, Papá?"

His father had lifted the oxygen mask from his face, smiled, and whispered, "At first. Not anymore."

Hector could not imagine the kind of courage it took to

face death like that. When he'd thought he was going to die in Joey's choke hold, he'd panicked—worse than panicked, if there could be such a thing. Now he had to live knowing that Joey would kill him tomorrow, the day after, sometime. And how could he not be afraid to die? Hector covered his face with a pillow. Joey had called him a worm, a gusano.

But if he was a worm, he wouldn't be feeling such shame.

The next morning, Hector made up his mind to put on his best "nothing happened" face. There was no way he was going to make things worse by letting his family know about the Joey incident. His mother and Aurora would insist on going to the police. Fili would not hesitate to confront Chavo and Joey. So Hector would keep the incident—and his cowardice—to himself. Maybe he would tell Azi, but he needed to think about that. Fili had already left for work when he got up, changed bandages, and got dressed. He took a deep breath and walked out of his room.

His mother waved at him from the living room. "That was Mrs. Poormaddi," she said to Hector, hanging up the phone. "She was calling to congratulate me about your award. You got first place and Azi got second. There's a banquet next week, and we're all going to go together."

Hector sat on the sofa. He was exhausted from a sleepless

night. "It's Mrs. Pourmohammadi, not Mrs. Poormaddi," he told his mother. Then, realizing what she'd said, he asked, "What award?"

Aurora came out of the kitchen with a large wooden spoon in her hand. "The Lions gave you an award for an essay you wrote. You got five hundred dollars, and Azi got two hundred. Remember those new basketball sneakers you promised me for my birthday? The ones you never got for me?"

"How do you know all this?" their mother asked. "Mrs. Poormaddi didn't mention anything about any money."

"It's in the letter that Hector got." Aurora walked to the kitchen table and picked up a white envelope.

Hector stood up, making sure he didn't wince at the pain in his chest. He walked slowly toward Aurora and snatched the envelope from her hand. "You're opening my mail now?"

"I'm sorry. I got carried away. I just knew it had to be good news."

Hector gave her a quick frown and began to read. The Lions Club was informing him that his essay on "The Pursuit of Happiness" had won first place. He and his family were invited to the luncheon/banquet where the first-, second-, and third-place winners would read their essays and receive trophies and cash prizes.

Hector remembered how Azi had pestered him to enter the contest. He'd written the essay hurriedly during study period and then had given it to Azi after she'd asked him if she could read it. That was the last time he'd seen it.

"Azi must have sent it," Hector said to himself.

"Actually, it was *moi*," Aurora said. "So, basketball sneakers?"

"Aurora," Mami said with motherly firmness, "some of that money—not all of it, but some of it—will go to pay over-due bills. Will that be okay with you, Hector?"

Hector nodded quickly at his mother and then grabbed Aurora before she disappeared into the kitchen.

"What do you mean *moi*?" he asked her. "*You* sent the essay?"

"Correctomundo! I did it! Azi came by one afternoon to return your essay when you had gone to Zaragoza with Fili to get a haircut. She gave me the essay and told me I should read it because it was beautiful and because it was about Papá. Then she told me to make sure you sent it and even gave me a stamped envelope with the Lions' address. I knew you probably wouldn't do it, so I looked for the essay on your laptop and fixed the typos that Azi had underlined and then I printed it and sent it in. I told Azi not to tell you I'd done it."

"Aurora, that was such a nice thing to do!" Mami pulled Aurora to her and gave her a warm hug. "Wasn't that nice of your sister, Hector?"

"You should have asked me," Hector said, and winced. He touched his chest.

"You okay?" Aurora asked.

Hector nodded, then tugged at her ponytail to let her know she was forgiven.

"Ouch! You wouldn't have sent it even if I'd asked you! You say things about Papá in there that you're way too shy to talk about. It's a good essay. Sad but good."

Aurora was right. Something had happened to him while he was writing it—a sadness that had been bottled up began to flow.

"Come here, Hector." Mami opened her arms, and Hector allowed himself to be hugged. "Your papi would be so proud of you. I can't wait to hear what you say about him. But I'm going to wait until the banquet."

Hector wriggled out of his mother's arms. "It's on a Saturday, and I work on Saturdays. Fili works too. Maybe they can just send us the check?" Walking outside all dressed up in front of Joey's hateful stare was the last thing he needed.

"Don't even start, Hector," his mother said. "We are all going to the banquet. You tell your manager when you see him tomorrow to change your shift to Sunday for next week. Fili will ask Manny to give him the day off."

"And we'll all pile into Fili's truck," Hector said.

"Don't you worry about any of the detalles. Mrs. Poormaddi got it all figured out. She called Mr. Lozano and he's going to pick us all up in the school van."

"Mami, what will I wear?" Aurora asked, worried.

"We'll make some alterations to your confirmation dress..."

"No way! That ugly thing! Mami, no one wears stuff like that anymore."

"We can discuss this later. Right now, I think you have some potatoes that need peeling." She turned to Hector. "We'll have to find you a suit somewhere. Maybe I can fix your father's brown suit."

"For a luncheon all you need is a white shirt and a tie." Hector said this quickly and with as much authority as he could muster.

"You sure?" Mami sounded doubtful. "It's a luncheon banquet, after all."

"Absolutely. Shirt and tie. I'm a hundred percent sure." Hector hurried down the hall to his room. He got in, closed the door behind him, and exhaled. He went to stand by the window that separated his bed from Fili's. Outside, Chavo and his friends sat on dilapidated patio chairs drinking and smoking. A car stopped in front of the group, and Chavo got up, leaned into the driver's open window, and exchanged a small plastic bag of white powder for cash.

Hector pulled out the chair to his desk and sat. He thought about calling Azi. He had betrayed her by giving Joey her name, her full name. Should he warn her? But telling her about Joey would also mean revealing what a coward Hector was.

By the ditch the day before, Joey had said something about Azi being too hot for a pendejo like him. Hector wondered: Could you think of your best friend as hot and still be best friends? It wasn't as if he didn't notice her hotness. He'd have to be blind not to. It's just that she was so much fun to talk to and so much fun to be with and so much fun to argue with. Why risk ruining that with some attempt at romance? Romance complicated things with its intensity. It turned what was carefree and easy into jealousy, possessiveness, obsession. That was Hector's experience, although he had to admit, his experience with girls was limited to an eighth-grade crush on the beautiful Becky Duggan. That romance had gone exactly nowhere. Besides, Azi was totally dedicated to her studies and her plan for the future. She was brilliant. She was right when she said that she was smarter than him. Last year, her science project about the effects of ginger on the autoimmune disease lupus had won first place in the whole state of Texas. She had time for a best friend but not for a boyfriend. Azi routinely told interested guys that her mother would not let her date until after high school.

Hector had asked her once if this was true. Did her mother really prohibit dating?

"Yes" had been Azi's response. Then, "More or less."

"What does that mean?" Hector had asked.

"It means that it's not an unbreakable, hard-and-fast rule. It's a good rule for now. More or less."

And that had been that.

Hector had brought himself to believe that it was a good rule . . . more or less. It kept each of them focused on their respective future plans while having the benefit of a true friend who cared for you and pushed you when you needed pushing.

Like her push to write the essay on the pursuit of happiness, which had now made him and his family five hundred dollars richer. If only he didn't have to stand up in front of people and read all those things he'd written about his father. Private things. Things he had never shared with anyone, not even with his brother. Fili, who had not been the same person since Papá died. Fili, who worried everyone with his quiet, constant drinking. Fili, who had been Papá's best friend. Fili, who'd sit with Papá in the backyard and read to him from old *National Geographic*s. Fili, who was truly brave.

A memory suddenly came to Hector. The week after they'd moved into the projects, Fili was washing his truck on the street in front of their apartment. Hector was helping him.

Chavo and Joey walked over from the end of the street where they'd been sitting.

"Fifty-eight?" Chavo asked.

Fili was kneeling, cleaning the front tire with a brush. Hector was holding a hose they had hooked up to a faucet on the side of the building. "Fifty-six," Fili responded without looking up. Chavo peered inside the truck's cabin. Joey stared at Hector.

"How much you want for it?" Chavo asked.

Fili looked up briefly, smiled. "I'm not selling it."

"Maybe you should." The tone was still friendly, but Hector was sure he heard a hidden threat.

Fili stood, took the hose from Hector, rinsed the tire carefully. Then, as if surprised that Chavo was still there, he turned to him and said, "I'm not selling *you* the truck." The words were spoken softly, but Hector heard the slight but unmistakable emphasis on the word *you*. Joey moved closer to Fili, but Chavo stopped him with a small movement of his hand. Fili and Chavo kept their eyes calmly on each other. Neither one showed animosity or fear. If anything, it almost seemed to Hector as if Fili hoped that Chavo would start something.

After a while, Chavo said, "If you change your mind, you know where I live." Then he turned around and walked back to the courtyard. Joey winked at Hector before following his brother.

"Why'd you do that?" Hector asked Fili when they were down the street.

"Do what?"

"You shouldn't disrespect those guys. Aren't you afraid of them?"

Fili looked at Hector for the longest time. Finally, he said, "If you show fear, they'll take advantage of you."

"Like dogs, you mean. If they smell fear, they'll bite you."

"It's different with dogs and people. Dogs can smell fear even if you don't show it. But with people, sometimes it's enough if you don't show it."

Hector snapped out of the memory. What would Fili say about the fear he'd shown Joey? He needed to think about other things, try to get back to some kind of normal. He studied the chessboard on his desk. He had been re-creating the third game between Boris Spassky and Bobby Fischer at the 1972 world championship in Reykjavík, Iceland. Hector wanted to understand Spassky's and Fischer's reasons behind every move. Within the universe of those sixty-four squares there was nothing that could not be understood with the proper application of thought. The position of the pieces on the board reflected Fischer's eleventh move, when Fischer had moved his black knight to a square on the side of the board away from all the action. There was no apparent rhyme or reason for the move, and yet, it turned out to be the beginning of Spassky's defeat.

Hector pushed the chessboard to a corner of the desk. It was a sad day when even chess could not keep his mind from the C on his chest. Automatically, without thinking, he opened his laptop and checked the messages folder in the Maestro I website. One of the few things that Azi did not know about him was that he did not just "play chess against a robot," like she put it. On Maestro I, Hector could match skills against a computer program that could play at levels from beginner to grandmaster, or he could compete against other players from anywhere in the world. Most of the time, the matches were played without the players revealing anything about themselves. Players knew the level of their play by how Maestro I ranked them, but little else. They could send messages to each other as they played, but the comments were usually limited to impersonal statements like "Ouch!" or "Great move!"

The week before, Hector had gotten a message from Elbereth, the player he had just beaten. Hector decided to read the message again now. He knew that she was brilliant by the way she played, but he also imagined that with a name like Elbereth, she had to be beautiful. He found the message and read:

ELBERETH:

Hey, Chaturanga! Nice going! Where did you learn that trap with the rook and the stupid pawn? I thought I had you when I captured your two knights and then whamo! You killed me. This is my first loss in Maestro. I'm totally humiliated!

CHATURANGA:

You shouldn't be. You play brilliant. I thought you found my trap when you hesitated taking my second knight.

ELBERETH:

I knew it was too good to be true. I never in a million years imagined you'd move the rook. He was your king's only protection! God, I hate losing to guys! But you're like a complete chess player, so I shouldn't feel too bad, right?

CHATURANGA:

How did you know I was a guy?

ELBERETH:

I don't know. I just assumed. What woman would choose to be named after the four ancient divisions of chess: infantry, cavalry, elephantry, chariotry? It's a tiny bit arrogant, but just the kind of name a guy would choose, don't you think?

CHATURANGA:

Arrogant? You mean like naming yourself after an elven goddess in The Lord of the Rings? ;) By the way, confidence is not arrogance.

ELBERETH:

Ouch! Well said, Chaturanga. I like your style. Can I ask you a personal question? How old are you?

CHATURANGA:

16. You?

ELBERETH:

Just turned 18. My birthday was last week.

CHATURANGA:

Happy birthday. Mine is coming up next month.

ELBERETH:

So, do you do anything else for fun besides chess? Sports? Friends?

CHATURANGA:

A little basketball. I also like to work on my
truck. I have a '56 Chevy. I have a part-time job
at a grocery store. That and school take up all
my time. How about you? You very social?

ELBERETH:

No. I'm kind of a loner actually. I read a lot.
There's not much of a social life here in Amarillo.
Where do you live?

CHATURANGA:

I live in El Paso. Hey, we're in the same state at
least.

ELBERETH:

At least. Listen, Chaturanga. My mom is calling
me. We're having a girls' night out at Pizza Hut.
Keep in touch? You owe me a rematch.

CHATURANGA:

Yes. Absolutely. It was a pleasure beating
you . . . I mean, getting to know you.

He had read the exchange maybe ten times since it had taken place, and he still felt that there was more to discover about Elbereth in the words she had chosen to use. One thing for sure, she was interested in him. He berated himself for lying. He was barely sixteen. His birthday was last month. And the stuff about owning and liking to work on his 1956 Chevy truck . . . Where the hell had that come from? It was pathetic. What about that line *confidence is not arrogance*? Who but a corny nerd would say something like that?

After the online exchange, he had searched his three-volume set of *The Lord of the Rings*. Maybe understanding the name Elbereth could give him a better picture of the person who chose it. The elves in the Shire sing a song in her praise and then later, when Frodo is attacked by the Ringwraiths at Weathertop, he calls out to Elbereth for help. The word meant "Star Kindler" or "Lady of the Stars." It was a name uttered like a prayer, which made the girl behind the name, the girl who had called him a "complete chess player," even more mysterious and alluring. And it went without saying, that only a physically beautiful girl would choose that name.

A few times since that one and only virtual conversation, he had sat with his fingers poised over the keyboard ready to

33

send Elbereth a message but had never gone through with it. It was weird, but he felt somehow disloyal to Azi. Azi was a great chess player, as good as Elbereth, and on the way back home from school, she was about to call him a chess genius before she decided not to use the g-word. A genius was better than a complete player any day, wasn't it? So why was it easier to crush on Elbereth, an online fantasy, than on Azi, the flesh-and-blood girl who was also his best friend?

If only human emotions were as easy to understand as chess moves.

CHAPTER 4

I t was 5:00 p.m. later that day. Hector was lying in bed reading the latest text from Azi when he heard the rattling of Fili's truck. That morning, he'd texted Azi and told her that he wasn't feeling well. They would have to postpone their basketball practice. Now Azi was asking how he was and whether she could come over. Hector stood and went to the window. He watched his brother get out of the truck and open the hood. Down the street, Joey parked the blue Impala in front of his apartment. He came out of the car alone and looked briefly in the direction of Fili's truck, which was still running. Fili closed the hood gently. Joey plopped down on an old sofa and lit a cigarette.

Hector grabbed his phone and sat at his desk. He was not ready to see Azi. She would know that something had happened. He was not going to be able to hide the Joey incident from her, but he wasn't ready to talk about it. He texted back.

I'm okay, really. Some kind of stomach bug. I'm not very nice to be around. Tomorrow?

He waited a few minutes and read.

Okay. Feel better. Oh, and congratulations on your essay!

The essay. He had spent the day sleeping and reading chess books and feeling like crap and had not thought about the famous essay. He searched in his laptop for a copy and found it in a folder titled *Odd Stuff* and began to read it. The sadness that he had felt when he wrote the piece came back to him. He remembered what Aurora had said about the essay: "Good, but sad." He read a few more lines looking for the good, but all he could see was the sad. He closed the document and listened to the joyful voices of Aurora and his mother. They were glad to see Fili. It was unusual for him to come home in time for dinner, especially on a Saturday night.

Hector stared at the small bookcase in front of the desk. Fili and he were supposed to share its shelves, but Fili kept the only book he ever read on the nightstand next to his bed. Hector looked at it now, a worn copy of *Automotive Service: Inspection, Maintenance, Repair* that Hector had given Fili for his twenty-second birthday. Brand-new, the book cost over two hundred dollars, but Hector had found a used copy of the first edition from an online bookdealer for only twenty-five dollars plus shipping. Hector had tried to read one of the chapters once, but the language was as inscrutable to him as his chess books were to Fili.

"Way to go, carnal!" Fili said, opening the door to their room. "Mami just told me about the award and the banquet." Hector felt Fili's hands on his shoulders. He turned to watch Fili sit on the edge of his bed and begin to unlace his work boots.

"You going out tonight?" Hector asked.

"Not just me," Fili said, throwing a dirty sock at Hector. "You and me. We're going out. To celebrate. I just got the okay from Mami."

Hector carefully lifted the sock from his lap with two fingers and dropped it on the floor. "You and me?"

"As soon as I shower. We'll get something to eat at Pepe's and play a couple of games of pool. We'll make a night of it. You need to go out. Have a little fun." Fili took off a white T-shirt smudged with grease.

"Have a little fun?"

"What?"

"Aurora put you up to this, didn't she?" Hector looked in the direction of the kitchen, where Aurora and Mami were now arguing.

"No," Fili said. "Maybe. A little. Okay, she called me at work and ordered me to come home and take you out. But I wanted to also." Fili smiled guiltily.

"We can't let that little tyrant rule our lives," Hector said, pretending to be upset.

Fili laughed. "Can't be done, even if we wanted to."

"Listen, tonight's not a good night. I'm not feeling all that great."

"Mami says you've been locked up in here all day. It will be good for you to get out. Just for a couple of hours. You need to change or anything?"

Hector looked at Fili. How long had it been since he'd seemed so happy? He pulled the chair away from his desk and said, "Okay, but I'm not changing. This is good enough for your usual hangouts."

"Ha, ha. Funny," Fili said as he walked out of the room.

Half an hour later, they were climbing into Fili's truck.

"Shoot," said Fili.

"What?" Hector asked.

"I don't have any money."

"Didn't you get paid today?"

"I gave my paycheck to Mami when I came in."

"Why don't we just have dinner at home? We can go out some other day. We need your paycheck for the bills."

"Bills can wait. I'll be right back." Fili jumped out of the car.

Hector saw Joey still sitting on the old sofa. Two girls and another boy were gathered on ratty patio chairs around him. One of the girls stood up and pointed her finger at the boy's face. She stumbled and fell into his lap. Everyone laughed.

Hector moved his arm up ever so slowly and locked his door. He looked for a way to roll up his window without being noticed, but the handle that cranked up the glass was rusty and there was no way to do it without Joey noticing.

It was too late anyway. Joey raised his hand and made a C with his thumb and index finger.

Hector's heart was still beating hard when Fili opened the door to the truck. "You all right?"

"Yeah. Why wouldn't I be?"

Fili started the truck, made a U-turn, and drove slowly away. When they were out of the projects, Fili said, "Maybe tomorrow night we can go to the church's parking lot and you can practice driving."

"I have to study for a geometry test on Monday," Hector said.

Fili pulled to the side of the road and stopped. He eased the clutch in and said, "Go ahead, put it in first."

Hector stretched his arm and rested his left hand on the vibrating knob of the gearshift that rose from the floor of the truck. He jiggled the gearshift sideways to make sure it was neutral and then pushed up. The engine made a hard grinding noise, sputtered, and died. A car behind them honked.

"It's no use," Hector said. "We should get a car everyone can drive." Immediately, he regretted saying that. The truck was Fili's joy. And it had been Papá's joy as well. The memory of Papá and Fili working on it came to Hector. Hector reached out and patted the stick shift. "Sorry," he said. "I didn't mean that."

Fili started the engine again and eased the gearshift smoothly into first. The car behind them honked again. Fili moved as far to the right of the road as he could and motioned with his hand for the car to pass. "Nah, Mami thinks so too," Fili said. "She wants me to sell the truck, get something automatic that you can drive and later Aurora. It makes sense, don't you think?" Hector could sense a note of sadness in Fili's voice.

"Aurora and I can learn to drive this," Hector said. "How hard can it be if even a dummy like you can do it?"

Fili laughed. He always laughed easily when Hector or Aurora teased him.

"So," Fili said, "I know I probably won't understand it. But what was this writing about that you won an award for? Aurora said it was about Papá."

Hector braced himself on the dashboard as Fili slammed on the brakes. The car that had honked at them had stopped in the middle of the road. A young woman about Fili's age came out of the rear passenger door and ran to Fili's side of the truck. She wobbled as if she were drunk. She handed Fili a folded piece of paper, giggled, and then ran back to the car. Fili opened the paper, glanced at it quickly, as if he knew what he would find, and tucked it in the front pocket of his shirt. He waited for the car in front to gain some distance before moving again.

"Phone number?"

Fili shifted gears and moved on slowly, letting the car with the girls gain some distance. "Silly girls," he said.

"Do you ever call any of them?" It was not the first time Hector had seen a "silly girl" give his brother her phone number.

"Sometimes," Fili admitted, embarrassed. Then, "But not for a while."

Hector sighed. He imagined what it would be like if he were as popular with girls as his brother was. Better yet, what if he were as fearless as Fili? Nothing scared him, nothing ever seemed to weigh on his mind. Nothing, except Papá's death.

"Tell me about this writing you did," Fili said. Then, when Hector remained lost in thought, he continued. "Mami and Aurora are really excited about the banquet next week."

"The famous banquet," Hector said. "Mami's going to make you wear Papá's brown suit. You'll roast to death in it."

This time Fili did not laugh, and Hector knew what Fili was thinking. Papá only had two suits: the green cotton suit he had been buried in and the heavier brown suit. Their mother had chosen the green suit for the open casket because she thought it made Papá look peaceful.

"That's okay," Fili said. "It will be like Papá is there listening to you."

They didn't say anything else the rest of the way. Fili turned into the parking lot of Pepe's and shut off the ignition. "You're not going to drink too much, are you?" Hector asked, remembering the last time the two of them had come to Pepe's.

"I'll be good. Don't worry," Fili said, smiling. "Come on, let's go celebrate."

Pepe's Cantina was a minefield of memories for Hector. It was the place Papá had liked to go after work. That was before Mami put her foot down and said that if he was going to continue drinking, he would have to do it at home. She bought him the most expensive tequila and the best Mexican beer, and Papá stayed at home and sipped his beers and tequila until he fell asleep. He drank in the backyard of their old house whether it was hot or cold with a little transistor radio playing Mexican music by his side. If you sat next to him, he would talk to you about growing up in Las Peñitas, a ranch in the state of Chiapas, Mexico.

Fili was the member of the family who most enjoyed Papá's stories. Around the time when Fili was Aurora's age, Papá started pouring some of his beer into Fili's plastic glass. After a while, Fili was sitting with his father, drinking openly. Mami complained a little but soon gave up. Hector understood why she did it. Those two needed each other. They were like two ships held in place by the anchor of time they spent together.

Hector was not surprised that first Papá and now Fili liked coming to Pepé's. There was something quietly cheerful about the place. In many ways, it reminded Hector of their living room back home, the home they'd lost, with its purple tablecloths and the little altar to the Virgen de Guadalupe on the wall. It was light enough to see who was there but dim enough so that you didn't feel as if people were looking at you. There was a big oak bar on one side of the room that reminded Hector of a Western movie, and whenever he saw it, he thought of asking for a glass of sarsaparilla, whatever that was. There was an open doorway next to the bar, and through it, Hector could see a room with an ornate red-felt billiards table that was so solid and so heavy-looking that Hector imagined Pepe had found it there one day and then built his restaurant around it. Uncomfortable gray folding chairs lined the walls of that room. The only other furniture was a tall table where billiard players put their beer bottles or glasses when they shot.

Fili walked over to a table in the corner of the main room

and waited for Hector to sit in one of the two chairs. It was the exact same table they had sat at the last time he'd come to Pepe's with Fili. Hector hesitated and then took the chair facing the door. Fili waved at the man behind the bar and sat down. "I think Pepe will put something in your Coke if we ask him," Fili said. "It's a special occasion. We're celebrating."

"Every day is a celebration for you," Hector responded. The words were not spoken with any kind of meanness, but Hector saw that they hurt Fili. His brother did not need any reminders that he was an alcoholic, just like Papá.

"Not every day," Fili said. "Mami made me promise to only drink mineral water on Sundays."

"Why?"

"To flush out my kidneys, she says."

A young woman stood by their table. She put a can of beer with half a lime on top in front of Fili. Hector could see her blush through her dark skin. She was smiling at Fili as if the two shared a secret.

"I didn't think you were coming today," she said.

"I went to get my brother. He won a big prize for some writing he did in school."

The young woman looked at Hector. "Really?"

It wasn't just Fili's words of praise that made Hector blush, it was also the striking beauty of the girl. It was a face that Hector had seen before, but where?

"Gloria, this is Hector. The smart little brother I told you about."

"Nice to meet you, Hector." Gloria's hand stood in front of him for a few seconds before Hector took it. It was cold and wet from the can of beer she had been holding.

"Hi," Hector muttered.

"Can I get you something to drink?"

Hector suddenly remembered where he had seen the girl before. On Zaragoza Road, in Chavo's blue Impala. There was no mistaking it. When he'd seen her there, he'd wondered how someone so beautiful could be interested in a criminal like Chavo.

"Hector, are you there?" Fili said, joking.

"Sorry," Hector said, managing to meet Gloria's eyes. "Do you have any lemonade?"

"Not exactly lemonade, but sometimes people drink margarita mix without the alcohol." After Hector nodded, she said, "Should I get menus?"

"Maybe Hector wants one," Fili responded. "I'll have the usual." The way Fili looked at Gloria, it was clear she was not just a girl who'd handed him her phone number. A sinking feeling came over Hector. If Fili was involved with Chavo's girlfriend ... that had to be the reason for Joey's sudden hatred. Damn. It couldn't be. Fili wouldn't put him, put all the family, in danger like that. Would he?

"I'll have whatever he's having," Hector said. Gloria nodded, then left . . . but not before smiling at Fili one more time. Hector had no idea what Fili's "usual" was, but he didn't care. The way he felt just then, food was the least of his concerns. He waited until Gloria had disappeared through a door next to the bar before leaning across the table and saying to Fili, "Please tell me you're not dating her."

Fili looked surprised by Hector's statement. After a few seconds of silence, Fili said, "Truth is, I was thinking of bringing you here even before I found out about the contest. I wanted to talk to you. To tell you about Gloria."

"So, you *are* dating her." Hector put his elbows on the table and grabbed his head. "Is it serious?"

"I love her, Hector. It's never happened before to me. And I don't think it will happen again with anyone else."

"God."

"What . . . what's the matter?"

Could Fili really be as clueless as he seemed? Hector couldn't believe it.

"Do you know who she is?"

"She's Gloria," Fili said, turning toward the swinging door by the bar where Gloria had disappeared.

"She's Chavo Mendez's girlfriend. You know that, right? You have to know that."

"Oh." Fili smiled, as if finally understanding why Hector was so worried. "Gloria doesn't go out with Chavo anymore. It's over."

Hector was tempted to unbutton his shirt and prove to Fili that it was far from over, when he saw Gloria walking toward their table with a can of beer in one hand and a tall green glass in the other. "Here you go," she said. "One Tecate and one virgin margarita." Hector kept his eyes fixed on Fili. He did not want to look at her. Gloria stood there, as if waiting for more.

"Thank you," Fili finally said. There was a tenderness in Fili, in his voice, in the way he looked at Gloria, that reminded Hector of the last weeks of Papá's life, when Fili would sit on a chair next to Papá's bed and read to him.

When Gloria had left again, Hector said, "You're in love." He didn't even try to sound happy.

Fili blushed and wrung his hands. Was that the first time that Hector had ever seen his brother blush?

"I never felt . . . this." Fili wrapped his hand around the beer can as if to squash it. "I'm cutting down on the drinking. Trying to anyway. No more than three beers a day for a couple of weeks. Two beers after that, then one. Gloria's helping me."

It was good. It was what Fili needed. Hector could feel a

mixture of anger and worry and also happiness for Fili. It was hard to choose one emotion over the others. Hector lowered his head in thought.

"I'm going to bring her to the house to meet Mami and Aurora. Tomorrow. What do you think?"

Hector was still thinking about Chavo. Maybe Chavo was not the violent monster Hector made him out to be. But Hector knew that was only wishful thinking. Joey was bad, and Chavo was worse. Hector remembered when Chavo had thrown the beer can at Fili's truck. The anger in Chavo's face.

"Hector! Earth to Hector!" Fili said, laughing, repeating one of Aurora's favorite phrases.

"What?"

"I'm bringing Gloria to the house tomorrow. For Sunday dinner. Mami will like her." Then, "I hope Aurora likes her."

"Aurora will be the real test," Hector admitted.

"Yeah." Fili raised the can and took a small sip. He licked the salt from his lips and then said, straightening up, "Hey, tonight is about you. Let's talk about that award. And what about your chess playing? Let's talk about your future."

"My future?" Hector echoed. "My future is the same as it's always been. Work hard in high school, get a scholarship to go to college." Hector was tempted to accuse Fili of obviously not giving a damn about his future. If he did, he would not go out with Gloria. But Fili seemed so at peace, so happy. Didn't he deserve that?

"You say that as if all that was no big deal. But it's a big deal, Hector. It's what Papá hoped for you. He always knew you were smart. It's why he wanted all of us to speak English at home, so you'd succeed in your future." Fili paused, and Hector felt his brother's pride in him. Then Fili said, smiling, "And . . . is there someone special in your future?"

Hector knew that Fili was asking about Azi. Fortunately, just then Gloria came with two plates of food, and the question went unanswered. Hector smiled when he saw the cheeseburger and french fries. He should have known that was Fili's "usual." Papá had liked to tease Fili about ordering cheeseburgers in Mexican restaurants. "Are you really my son?" Papá would joke.

"So what kind of award did you get?" Gloria asked.

Hector tried to keep his eyes on Gloria, but there was something about her that made it hard for him to look at her directly. Maybe it was her good looks that made him nervous, or maybe it was the feeling of imminent danger that he now associated with her. Hector looked at Fili as if it had been he who had asked the question. "The topic was the pursuit of happiness. The phrase 'pursuit of happiness' comes from the Declaration of Independence. The Lions Club sponsored the contest. Aurora, my little sister, sent it in without my consent." Hector wished he hadn't mentioned the Declaration of Independence. And he shouldn't have used the word *consent*. He was sure he had just sounded like a big snob.

"Wow," said Gloria. Fili's face radiated with pride. "Do you think there's any chance that I could read what you wrote? American History was my favorite class in high school. I liked all that stuff about the Civil War."

Hector looked at Gloria and then quickly turned away. Did she think that the Declaration of Independence was a document from the Civil War?

"Sure," Hector said. "I'll give Fili a copy to give to you."

"Hector," Fili said, lighting up with an idea, "what if Gloria comes with us to your banquet next Saturday? Anyone can go, right?"

"What banquet?" Gloria raised her finger to let a woman at the next table know that she'd be right over.

"There's a banquet next Saturday where Hector will read what he wrote. We're all going. You want to come? Hector, she can come too, right?"

"It's not really a ban—" Hector tried to swallow, but his saliva got stuck in his knotted throat and he started to choke. Gloria hit him softly on his back with the palm of her hand.

"You okay?" Gloria asked, offering him the glass of margarita mix.

"Yes," Hector said. "Sorry."

"What do you think, Hector? Can Gloria come to the banquet next Saturday?"

"Sure," Hector said, not very convincingly.

"It'd be great if you could come. We can all go together," Fili said to Gloria.

Hector imagined Chavo sitting at the end of the street watching Gloria and Fili climb into the white school van. The irritation in his throat worsened, and he started coughing again.

"I'd love to,"Gloria said when Hector pulled himself together. Then to Hector,"Are you sure it's okay? What time?"The way she asked, Hector knew she must have sensed his apprehension.

"If you really want to," Hector added quickly. "It's not really a banquet. More like a luncheon. It's at one o'clock. But it's not the big deal that my family is making it out to be."

The faint smile on her face confirmed to Hector that she had sensed his reluctance. "Well, we can talk about it tomorrow when I come for dinner. Did Fili tell you?"

"Yes," Hector said.

"You'll get some real Mexican food," Fili said, as if to fill up the silence. "We'll eat around noon and then afterward we'll all go for a ride." Fili winked at Gloria.

"I can't wait." Gloria touched Fili's shoulder. "But you guys better eat—your burgers are getting cold."

Gloria moved to the next table, and Hector stared at his plate. Fili removed the top bun from the cheeseburger and began to pour hot sauce onto it. When he finished dousing the burger, he did the same to the french fries. Fili's look of total concentration as he ate was identical to Papá's.

"You're not hungry?" Fili asked Hector.

Hector picked up a french fry, took it halfway to his mouth, and then dropped it on the plate again.

"We should probably talk," Hector said.

Fili stopped just before biting into his cheeseburger. "Talk?"

"Does Chavo know about you and Gloria?"

Fili placed the cheeseburger on the plate. He wiped his hands on his T-shirt and left a slight pink smudge of hot sauce on the front. When Hector asked the question, he thought that Fili would laugh at him or call him a scaredy-cat, like when Hector refused to jump in the waters of the irrigation ditch. But Fili did not laugh at him or call him names. Fili disappeared inside himself as if looking for a place where he could find the answer to Hector's question. It seemed like a long time passed before he answered, "Yes, he knows. Gloria went out with him a few times, that's all. But the guy is still stuck on her. Gloria also works at a beauty shop, and he keeps going there and bringing her flowers. He calls her a lot too. Gloria told him she was seeing me and that it was serious. He still wants her. I can't say I blame him." A faint smile appeared on Fili's face. He was about to continue speaking, but Hector interrupted.

"And you're not afraid?"

Fili gazed at Hector in silence for a long time. Then he said softly, "A little. You always have to be a little afraid around guys like Chavo. People say he can be violent."

"As in, he's killed people."

"That's what people say. But he was never violent with Gloria. Didn't even raise his voice with her, Gloria says. He always respected her. She didn't know who he was when she first went out with him. When she found out, she stopped it."

Hector rubbed his forehead. Could it be true that Gloria didn't know how Chavo made a living? If you didn't live in the projects, you probably wouldn't know. And Chavo, unlike his brother, Joey, didn't look or dress like an obvious delinquent. It was possible for Gloria and Fili to believe that Chavo would not do anything. Only, Hector had hard evidence—evidence engraved in his chest—that it was not over. It seemed likely that Joey's hatred was but a pale reflection of Chavo's. "I want to believe that things will work out for you . . ."

"But?"

"Chavo and Joey are not like us. Maybe I know them better than you. What if they see your going out with Gloria as disrespect? They're big on respect. You gotta show them you fear them or else. What if they take it out on us? On me? On

Aurora? Or what if this thing with Gloria doesn't work out? What if something happens? The last time that things were going great for you, for all of us, Papá died—"

"And I started messing up. I know. I'm not as dumb as I look. I know about Chavo and Joey. What they're like. But Hector, we can't stop trying to be happy. Pursuing happiness. Like you said."

"Yeah."

"You asked me if I was afraid of Chavo. I'm afraid that Gloria is too good for me. That this happiness is all a big tease. I *am* afraid that something could happen to Mami or Aurora or to you because of Gloria or this guy Chavo. I won't let it. I promise you that." The gentleness in Fili's eyes was replaced with ferocity and determination. Fili waited for Hector's smile, and then he said, "Even if this guy is stubborn and wants to make trouble, why should we let him rule our lives? Not do what we want or need to do because we're afraid? We can't give in to bad people like that. What are Gloria and me supposed to do? Say, no, we can't love each other because Chavo doesn't want us to? Should Gloria and I give up on each other because we're afraid of Chavo?"

Hector thought of something he had read in one of his chess books: Sacrifice is the ultimate tactic in chess—the deliberate giving up of a cherished piece for survival or victory. There was a part of him that wanted to say, *Yes, that's precisely what you should do. You should give up on Gloria so we can all be happy.* But he didn't. He remained silent, and after a while, Fili said, "Hector, it's going to be okay. I'm going to show you something tomorrow that will make you feel better. Something that will show you that I'm aware of all the dangers that could happen and have taken steps to protect us, all of us. After Mass, we'll all go together. You'll see. Mañana." Fili raised his beer and waited for Hector to raise his glass.

"Mañana," Hector repeated, without enthusiasm.

CHAPTER 5

Mañana came too soon for Hector. It seemed as if he had just finally fallen asleep when he heard Aurora's voice.

"Get up, Hector. We're going to Mass and then shopping!"

Hector opened his eyes wide and sat upright in his bed. "What time is it?" He stretched out and checked the alarm clock on the nightstand. "Seven fifty-five?"

"We're going to nine o'clock Mass today because after that—"

"We're going shopping. Got it." He started to push the sheet from him, and then he remembered the C on his chest. He covered himself again. "Would you get out of here, please? I need to get dressed."

Aurora sat on the edge of the bed. "You think I haven't seen you in your boxer shorts? Guess what—I'm getting a new dress today. For the Lions banquet next week. Fili and I talked Mamá out of fixing my confirmation dress."

Hector rubbed both his eyes. There was a slight chance

that he was still sleeping and that this and the past two days were only a bad dream. But when he opened them again, Aurora was still there, grinning, and his chest still throbbed. Hector made as if to speak, but before he could think about what he wanted to say, Aurora was talking again.

"The bad part is that I won't have hardly any time to shop because we have to be back here in time to have Sunday dinner with Gloria."

"You know about Gloria?" Hector asked.

"Yes."

"And Mamá?"

"Mmm-hmm. We got it out of Fili when we noticed he wasn't drinking so much anymore. There had to be a love reason behind that. A woman kind of knows these things. I'm sorry, Hector—Fili wanted to tell you himself."

"Well, he told me all right."

"Have you ever seen Fili so happy? He's like on a cloud. He said you met Gloria when you went to Pepe's. What's she like? Is she nice? Pretty?"

"Yes," Hector said. "Nice. Pretty."

"But? You didn't like her?"

"It's not that."

"Come on, Hector! Tell me."

Hector looked at Aurora for a few moments. Should he ruin her hopes with his concerns about Gloria and Chavo?

No. Let her be happy for Fili. At least for a while. "It's just that Fili is so serious about her. I've never seen him this serious about anyone else. It's scary how fast this is happening."

"Come and get it! Chilaquiles!" It was Fili from the kitchen.

"You didn't try to discourage Fili from going out with Gloria? I know how you can be, Hector, with your analytical whatever of all possible doom-and-gloom scenarios."

"No. I controlled myself. Now get out, please. I need to get dressed."

"Did she seem like a good girl? Not cheap-looking or cheap-acting or anything? Will she pass the Conchita test?"

"Yes. I mean no. Not cheap-looking. Nice. Mami will like her. She's very Mexican."

"Awesome. Fili really loves her, doesn't he?"

"He seems to."

"And did she look like she loved him?"

Hector shrugged. "I guess." How would he know what love looked like?

Gloria and Fili sat on one side of the table. On the other side sat Hector and Aurora. Mami, as usual, was at the head. Hector sat picking at his plate, surprised at how quickly Gloria had won over his mother. The minute she'd come in the door and smelled the mole sauce, she'd disappeared with Mami into the kitchen talking recipes . . . and that was that. It was Aurora who had taken up the motherly role of interrogation.

"So how did you two meet?" Aurora asked Gloria.

Gloria stopped folding a tortilla. She glanced at Fili before answering, "At Pepe's. I started working there in the evening after I finished at the beauty shop. They needed an extra waitress for Friday nights. That was four months ago. Now I work there on Thursdays, Fridays, and Saturdays. I met Fili the first Friday I was there."

"He asked you out *that night*?" Aurora blurted.

Gloria and Fili laughed at the same time. Gloria placed her hand on top of Fili's, said, "Not that night. I had to wait a few Fridays after that."

"But you probably get tons of guys hitting on you. Why Fili?"

"Aurora!" Mami warned. "Please watch your language. Gloria's our guest."

"To hit on someone is not bad language, Mami. It's regular young-people talk," Aurora explained.

"I know what hitting someone means," Mami responded. "I'm not so old that I don't understand. I watch your silly shows with you, don't I? And believe it or not, men hit me still . . . now and then. It's still not a respectful thing to ask."

"You mean men hit *on* you, not men hit you," Aurora said, trying not to laugh. Then, turning to Gloria, "I didn't mean to be disrespectful. It's just that you're so pretty."

"Thank you," Gloria said to Aurora with affection. Gloria turned to look at Fili, as if studying him. "Why Fili? He's just different. He didn't hit on me, as you say. He was just himself, and I was drawn to him. He seemed, I don't know, transparent. Like I could see his heart and it was pure."

Aurora's rare silence told Hector that she was now convinced that Gloria was the right person for Fili. And Hector had to admit that it was a good answer. Gloria's words described Fili perfectly. There was something "pure" about Fili even though Hector had never connected that word to Fili before. Hector, who had been having trouble looking directly at Gloria all night, gazed up at her now. She was a lot smarter than he had imagined, and seemed elegant in a simple and honest way. She wore no makeup other than lip gloss. Her nails were short and unpainted. Her hair was pulled back into a simple ponytail that made her age seem more like sixteen than twenty-one. But all the good things that Hector heard and saw in Gloria could not erase the one doubt he had about her. How could she ever go out with someone like Chavo?

After dinner, Hector and Aurora were in the kitchen washing the dishes when Gloria walked in.

"I want to help," she said.

"No way! You're the guest!" Aurora objected.

"Fili and your mother are looking for old photo albums. I thought maybe I could talk to Hector."

"Oh," Aurora said, catching on. "Yeah. Here." She handed Gloria a white dish towel. "I better make sure they don't take out any embarrassing pictures."

Hector was suddenly flustered. Why did Gloria want to talk to him? Had Gloria read any doubts on his face? He handed Gloria a dish, and she dried. Hector racked his brain for something to say. To his great relief, Gloria spoke first.

"You were very quiet at dinner."

The fork that Hector was cleaning slipped through his hands and splashed water from the sink on Gloria's dress. "I'm sorry. I got you all wet."

"Are you worried about Chavo?" Gloria asked, patting her dress with the dish towel.

"Fili told you?"

"He did. But he didn't have to. I noticed it on Friday when you came to Pepe's. You didn't want me to go the banquet. You were afraid Chavo might see me with your family?"

Hector blushed, embarrassed. "Sorry."

"No, don't be sorry. I understand." She sighed. "It's not as if we can ignore who Chavo is or what he does." Gloria waited for Hector to look at her. "I broke up with Chavo a month after I started going out with him. A friend who lives here told me what he was into. I asked him if it was true, and he admitted it. He said he had a plan to get out of the business. He was winding it down. But I told him that night that I couldn't see him anymore."

"And he was okay with that?"

Gloria hesitated before answering. "I think he saw it as something temporary. That I would come back to him when he stopped dealing. I explained to him that it wasn't just what he did, it was who he was. Anyone who didn't care about how he was hurting others, I mean, how could I ever love someone like that?"

"Does Chavo know about Fili?"

"I'm sure."

"And?"

"I don't know. I don't talk to him. When he calls, I don't answer. When he shows up at Pepe's or the beauty shop, I ignore him."

Gloria saw the worry on his face. She took the plate from his hand and spoke with strength and confidence. "The thing you need to know is that what Chavo cares the most about is making money. He has a good thing going, and he isn't going to do something stupid like pick a fight with a resident. That would call attention to him and mess up his business.

These projects are his territory. He's going to protect that at all costs."

That at least made some sense to Hector. Everyone knew that there was a secret agreement between the projects' security police and Chavo. He could sell his drugs as long as there were no violent crimes that would attract the attention of the regular police.

"There's a nice, caring side to Chavo, believe it or not," Gloria continued. "I know people say he's violent, but I never saw that side of him. Even now, I believe he cares about me. I don't believe he's capable of harming me or Fili."

Hector opened his mouth and was about to tell her about Joey. He was convinced that Gloria and Fili's relationship was the reason for Joey's attack. But if he told her about Joey, Fili would do something and then Joey would have an even greater reason to kill him. He couldn't take that chance. Let Gloria believe that Chavo was an angel. Hector bit his lips and tried to smile.

"You don't agree?" Gloria asked.

Hector shrugged. "I hope you're right. I just . . . I don't . . . I'm sorry, I can't imagine what you ever saw in Chavo."

"No need to apologize. I've asked myself that question many times. He was nice to me. Had a nice car. Gave me lots of presents. Helped my brother with a loan when he was out of work. He was respectful with my mother and father. Other girls envied me. I was flattered. And, like I said, Chavo kept his business separate from me. When I asked him what he did, he said he was a real estate broker. Maybe I was just being naive, I don't know." Gloria dried a plate in silence, and then she said, "There were little things about him that I should have picked up on right away. He always decided where we went to eat, what movie to watch, never asked me what I wanted to do. It was like he owned me."

I own you. Hector remembered Joey's words. He knew what it felt to be owned. He reached into the sink and pulled out the plug. Then he watched the soapy water swirl down. "Thank you for telling me all this," he finally said.

"You don't think I'm a bad person?"

"No, I never thought that. I can see what Chavo does from my bedroom window. That's why I'm worried."

"I understand. Don't worry. Fili's not one to wait for bad things to happen. Me neither. We're taking steps to make sure your worries don't come true."

There was an aura of certainty and confidence in the way Gloria spoke, and for a moment, Hector almost believed that things might turn out well.

Almost. But not quite.

CHAPTER 6

Gloria and Mami squeezed together in the cab of Fili's truck. Hector and Aurora sat on an army blanket in the back. Fili drove for fifteen minutes east on Alameda Avenue. They passed Socorro High School, and a mile or so later, Fili slowed down and turned onto a residential street. The houses were modest, one-story adobe-and-concrete-block houses with large well-cared-for yards. Two small boys, kicking a ball on the street, moved to the side as the truck went slowly by. A man and a little girl were painting a white mailbox with orange flowers. The man turned and waved at Fili. At the end of the street, Fili stopped.

Fili smiled from ear to ear when he saw the mystified look on the faces of his mother, sister, and brother. Fili opened the door, jumped out of the truck, and ran to the other side to let Gloria and Mami out. When they were all out of the truck, Fili, holding on to Gloria's hand, pointed at the house in front of them. Hector could tell it was an old house because—adobe bricks were visible in places where the yellow stucco had cracked. The grass in the front yard had brown spots from lack of watering, but it had been recently mowed and there was a bed of red and white roses on both sides of the stone path that led to the house. There was a large window next to the front door through which Hector could see that the house was not occupied. Mami walked over to examine the roses while Aurora reached and grabbed Gloria's hand.

"What is this, Filiberto?" Mami asked. "No more mysteries."

"Yeah, Fili. No more mysteries," Aurora repeated. Hector thought Aurora sounded like a child unwrapping a present.

Hope was beating on Hector's chest, desperately wanting to be let in. The house was too big for just Fili and Gloria. Could it be that they were all going to live here? No more Joey, no more beer cans on the stairs or smelly hallways. Socorro High School was down the street.

"Come on inside," Fili said, pulling keys out of his pocket.

Fili opened the green door, and Aurora rushed in. Hector waited for Mami, who was holding on to Gloria's arm. "Oh, God." Mami sighed. "This is too much for an old woman."

"Forty-eight is not old, Mami," Fili said. "Come inside and look."

Mami let go of Gloria's arm and walked quietly, solemnly, as if she were stepping into a church. "We had this kind of tile in the house I grew up in," Mami said, pointing at the floor. "It's genuine Mexican tile from Oaxaca."

"Just like you, Mami," Filiberto replied, kissing his mother on top of her head. "Genuine Mexican."

Aurora emerged from the hall, shouting. "You should see the backyard, Mami! It's like an orchard back there with all kinds of trees!" Aurora ran into the kitchen and out the back door.

Mami and Gloria followed Fili into the small kitchen. Mami ran her hand over the old gas stove. Then she turned and stood in front of the refrigerator. "I haven't seen one that was shorter than me in a long time."

Hector looked out the kitchen window and saw eight pecan trees lined in two rows of four. To the right of the trees, a few yards from the back porch, was a structure that looked like a separate garage. Aurora was out there peering through one of the windows. It had to be a house for all of them. But, wait, what if it was just for Fili and Gloria? He'd ask Fili if he could come live with them. He would tell him his life was in danger back in the projects. Hector tried to calm himself. If he could just summon the self-control he had when playing chess . . .

Mami opened the kitchen door, walked outside, and breathed deeply. She looked for the source of the fragrance and saw the clay pots with red geraniums. Mami sat on a wooden bench next to the geraniums. "Please tell me what this is all about," she begged Fili.

Fili and Gloria sat on a cinder-block ledge that separated the porch from the backyard. Hector found a bucket, turned it over, and sat down. They waited for Aurora, and when she came, she sat cross-legged on the concrete floor. All eyes were on Fili.

"The house used to belong to Manny's parents." Fili turned to Gloria. "Manny's my boss at the auto shop. He was my father's boss too and his good friend."

"Yes," Gloria said, smiling, "I know Manny."

"I'm sorry. I forget things," Fili said, putting his hand on top of hers. "Anyway, Manny's father built this house himself a few years after he came here from Mexico. Manny says his father was twenty-four when he built it. He was ninety-two when he died a couple years ago. Remember? We went to the funeral."

"I remember," Mami said.

Fili paused for a few moments, remembering, and then continued. "Manny's mother died five years ago, but his father, Don Hortencio, stayed here by himself. Don Hortencio was a carpenter, and that building there"—Fili turned to point at the garage-like structure—"was where he did his cabinet and furniture work. Manny put the house on the market about six months ago, but no one's been interested. It needs a lot of work."

"Fili, will you get to the point?" Aurora said impatiently.

Gloria gave Aurora a thumbs-up.

Fili laughed nervously. "Manny came up to me last week. I guess he saw me looking at an ad in the paper. Sears was looking for mechanics, and they pay four dollars an hour more than I get with Manny. Maybe he got scared to lose me. Papá and him were like brothers, you know. I don't even know how long Papá worked with Manny."

"Twenty years," Mami said.

"And I've been with him for two. So I told him I needed to make a little more." Fili stopped. He looked remorseful. "I told him that I had met a girl I liked a lot and that maybe it was time for me to get a place of my own." Fili looked into Gloria's eyes briefly.

"But not just a place for me," Fili added quickly, noticing the expression on Hector's face. "For all of us. Where we could all live together. Manny got worried. I'm his best mechanic. He told me to get in his car, and he drove me here. He said he could give me two dollars an hour more, and he would sell this house to us for eighty thousand dollars, twenty thousand less than he's asking. Then we drove over to the bank in Ysleta where Manny does business, and the man looked at the numbers and said the bank could give me a mortgage. All I need is sixteen thousand for a down payment."

Inside of Hector there was a big sigh of relief. The house was for all of them! For *all of them*!

But then reality hit. "Where are you going to get sixteen thousand dollars?" Hector asked.

"Excuse me, Hector," Mami said. "I need to ask Filiberto something first." Her eyes bored into Fili. "You and Gloria want to marry?"

Fili looked at Gloria and then at his mother. "With your blessing, Mamá, and with Gloria's father's blessing, that's what we want to do."

"Smart man," Aurora said.

"Aurora, please. No jokes right now." Mami was digging in her purse for a tissue.

"I think she's the one, Mami. I . . . know she is. I feel about her the way Papá told me he felt about you . . . when he first met you . . . and how he felt for you even on the day he died."

Mami's eyes filled with tears. She nodded. She could not argue with that. Aurora stood and went to sit next to Mami on the bench.

"And I feel the same way about your son," Gloria said to Mami. "I want this to be a home for all of us."

Fili continued. "You know me—I've never been good at planning. But I figure that I can work on the house over the next couple of months. I'll come here after work. Then, if everything goes right, we can move here in the summer. Hector and Aurora can start at Socorro High next fall. You know that man that waved at us when we were coming in? That was Mr. Ruiz. His wife works in Ysleta at the post office, and she gets off at the same time you get off from work. She can bring you home. I can drop you off in the morning on my way to Manny's."

"Yes! I like the plan, Fili!" Aurora jumped up, unable to stay seated anymore. "Provided Mami likes it. We need to get out of that apartment. The projects are not a good place for me and Hector to be growing up. Right, Hector?"

"Yes," Hector said, hiding his excitement. "It's not a good place. But where are you going to get sixteen thousand dollars? And what are the monthly mortgage payments? Don't forget we'd have to pay real estate taxes and other expenses here. Did you take all that into account?"

"So, when would the wedding be?" Mami asked, ignoring Hector's questions.

"I was thinking maybe in June. It won't be a big wedding. We need to save to furnish the house and fix it up. As soon as the house is ready, we'll move in. Manny will rent it to us until we have enough for the down payment. Don't worry, Hector, I have a plan for that." Fili removed the wallet from his back pocket, opened it, and took out a card. He gave it to

Hector. "These are the numbers that the loan person at the bank worked out."

Hector studied the card. The monthly payment for the mortgage, after the down payment, was only two hundred dollars more than what they were currently paying for rent. He could get Frank to give him more hours at the store to help. "Wow," Hector said. It was as if something very heavy in his chest had suddenly sprung wings and left him. Then he remembered the down payment. "But . . ."

Fili cut him off. "I can get eighteen thousand for the truck. A man that comes to the repair shop offered me that much."

Everyone was silent. Then Aurora said what Hector was thinking. "But you love that truck, Fili. It was Papá's truck and yours."

"Papá's okay with me selling it." The way Fili said this, it was as if he had recently consulted with his father.

"Wait," Aurora said, breaking the somber mood that had descended on everyone. "There's only three bedrooms. I'm not sharing a bedroom with Hector."

Fili stood and held out his hand for Mami. When she was standing, he put his arm around her shoulder and pointed to the garage structure. "The carpentry shop already has a toilet and a sink. Putting in a shower will not be a problem." Then he walked over to the end of the porch. "I can build a little passageway from the end of the house here to the shop, and we will have an extra-big room. That will be your room, Mami, if you want it."

"Mami," Aurora said, "if I were you, I'd let Fili and Gloria have that room. We don't want them keeping us up at night."

"Aurora! Behave!" Mami scolded. "But she's right," she said to Fili. "You will need your privacy."

Hector turned toward a soft sound coming from the pecan trees. A rare breeze rustled the leaves.

And the breeze seemed to say: All will be well.

CHAPTER 7

The next day, instead of taking his usual seat in the back of Mr. Lozano's social studies class, Joey sat down next to Hector. Whenever Mr. Lozano wasn't looking, Joey glared at Hector.

That was enough for Hector to abandon his recently born hope that all would be well. He tried to ignore Joey. He stared at the clock on the wall. Five more minutes and he would see Azi. After they got back from Socorro, Hector called her and agreed to meet at the school's basketball courts right after the last class.

Joey had shown an interest in Azi. He'd asked for her name. Azi was now in the orbit of Joey's evil attention. So Hector had decided that, painful as it would be, he had to do two things to protect Azi from Joey.

First, he would tell her about the Joey incident. He owed her the truth. She was his best friend.

The second thing he had to do was not be seen with her.

Joey thought that he and Azi were boyfriend and girlfriend, and that, Hector believed, put Azi in danger.

The intercom made a high-pitched whiny sound, and Principal Candelaria's voice burst forth full of ever-present pep.

"Good afternoon, everyone! I have an important announcement. It gives me great pleasure to tell you all that our very own Hector Robles and Azi Pourmohammadi have won first place and second place respectively in the Lions Club annual essay contest. The theme this year was 'The Pursuit of Happiness,' a phrase that, as you know, appears in our Declaration of Independence. Hector's and Azi's essays were awarded first and second place from among three hundred entries submitted by sophomores from all the El Paso high schools. This is the first time any student from Ysleta High has won this prestigious award. And to have two students win first and second place is amazing! Hector and Azi will be honored Saturday at a special banquet, where they will read their essays. Congratulations, Hector and Azi! Have a great rest of the week, y'all!"

The bell rang, and Hector couldn't tell whether the hooting and clapping was for him or because the long Monday was finally over. Joey stood and bumped Hector with his hip. Hector looked up to see a smirking Joey slide his finger across his neck.

Damn, Hector thought. *Damn, damn.* He had been determined to disappear from Joey's radar . . . and now this.

Hector stood by his desk, hoping his heart would stop thumping. He pretended to search for something inside his backpack until he was certain Joey had left out the back door. He was about to leave when he saw Mr. Lozano motion for him to come up to the front.

"Hector," Mr. Lozano said, "congratulations. I'm looking forward to joining you on Saturday. I'm going to get a school van and can pick your family up at, say, twelve fifteen."

Hector imagined Joey sitting in the ragged sofa watching his family pile into the white van.

"That's all right. If we go, we can take my brother's truck."

"I've seen your brother's truck, Hector. It's a fifty-six Chevy antique with a cabin that barely fits two people. Don't worry, your mother and Azi's mother have made all the arrangements."

Hector hesitated, then admitted, "I told my mother that all I needed to wear was a white shirt and a tie."

"You don't have a suit?"

"No, sir." It was the truth. The only suit was his father's.

"I have an old blue jacket from my son that will fit you. I'll bring it on Saturday. You can wear it with khaki pants and a tie. You have a tie?"

"Yes, my father's."

"Good. You will honor your father by wearing his tie. And you will honor my son by wearing his jacket. I want you to keep that jacket. Rafael would want you to have it." Mr. Lozano's eyes suddenly moistened. Hector knew Mr. Lozano's son had been killed in Iraq.

Hector lowered his head and started to walk away.

"Hector?"

"Yes?"

"Don't forget the competition for captain of the chess team is after school today."

"No, sir." Captain of the chess team. The last thing Hector wanted was more notoriety, more ways to draw Joey's hatred.

"You can't hide your light under a bushel," Mr. Lozano said.

Hector gave Mr. Lozano a knowing smile and walked away. Mr. Lozano was a social studies teacher, the chess team's coach, and the minister of a tiny Protestant church. The famous light under the bushel was from the Bible, and Mr. Lozano had repeated the words to his students so many times that Hector had the whole verse memorized: *You are the light of the world. A city set on a hill cannot be hid. Nor do men light a lamp and put it under a bushel, but on a stand, and it gives light to all in the house.*

The first time Mr. Lozano had said that to him, Hector had gone home and looked up the word *bushel*. A bushel was a unit of measurement for grain or fruit or a container that could hold a bushel of something. It was a good place to hide a light, which was exactly what Hector needed to do now in order to survive.

Hector stopped and looked both ways before stepping out into the hall. Joey was not the type to stick around school one second longer than necessary, but it was good to be careful. The hallway was deserted except for a couple of students getting books out of lockers. Hector walked out the exit door that led to the basketball courts and froze. There, a few yards away, stood Joey talking to Azi. Hector's first instinct was to turn around and go back inside the school. Immediately after that, he felt shame for wanting to run and leave Azi alone with Joey. He stood, wavering, not knowing what to do or how to interpret what he was seeing. Azi was listening attentively to Joey. She had the "all business" face she always wore at school. She did not seem frightened, and Joey did not seem to be threatening her.

"Hector!" Azi said when she saw him. She walked over to Hector and handed him the basketball. "Ready."

Joey slowly walked up to Hector and gently touched the spot on his chest where he was marked. "Be seeing you," he hissed.

Azi grabbed Hector's arm and pulled him in the direction of the basketball courts.

"What was that about?" Hector said, looking back to make sure Joey was gone. "What did he want with you?" The tone was all wrong. He sounded as if it was all Azi's fault or as if Azi *liked* talking to Joey. Maybe Hector was just jealous. Or maybe the source of Joey's hatred was jealousy. He wanted Azi, and Hector was in the way.

"He's just another jerk."

"You looked pretty interested in what he was saying to you." He had to admit that it felt good to say that. It was steam being let out at the wrong person, but at least it was being let out.

"Hector, come on," Azi said.

But Hector couldn't stop himself. "What was he saying to you?"

"He was asking me if I had family in Las Cruces. He said he knew a girl there who had a name just like mine. He must have gotten my name from the announcement this morning. He said this Sasha person was supposed to be almost as beautiful as me. He thought maybe we were related. Some misguided effort at flirting, I guess, but I think he was high on something."

"You need to stay away from him." They had reached the basketball court, and Hector began bouncing the ball as hard as he could.

Azi grabbed the ball before it reached Hector's hands

and said, "Let's sit on the bleachers. I need to put my sneakers on." They walked side by side in silence. He took a deep breath. He tried to imagine what it would be like to not have Azi's friendship and the picture he came up with was not pretty. He'd be a sad, miserable human being without her. Still, he had to do what he could to protect her from Joey. He got himself ready to be honest, but then Azi said, "Do you want to talk now or after we practice?" Azi sat on the bottom bleacher and made room for him to sit next to her.

Hector sat. He placed the basketball on the ground and held it tight with his feet, as if the ball would choose to be someplace else, if it could. "How'd you know? That I wanted to talk to you?"

"I thought you'd want to tell me about your trip to Socorro! Your mother told my mother and my mother told me. That's soo wonderful! I'm happy for Fili, and I'm happy for you. You'll be out of the projects. What you always wanted!"

"Thank you." He steeled himself. "But that's not what I want to talk to you about."

"Then what?" She seemed to take in his face. "What's weighing on you?"

Hector took a deep breath. Then he slowly unbuttoned the top three buttons of his shirt. He opened his shirt and removed a gauze bandage. Most of the C was covered with a delicate layer of scab, but in some places small pinpricks of blood could still be seen.

"Oh," Azi whispered.

Hector looked straight ahead. He could hear his words coming out of his mouth, and they seemed to belong to someone else. "I was in the back of the store folding boxes when Joey came. He pushed me against the dumpster and choked me and then carved a C for *coward* on my chest. I did nothing while he was doing this. I was terrified. Azi, I did nothing."

"Hector—"

"Let me finish. All he said was . . . he asked me if I thought I was a big mierda." Hector looked to see if Azi recognized the word. She did. "He said he was going to kill me. Not then but sometime. Maybe next week. Maybe next year. That he wanted me to be thinking about and waiting for it."

"God."

"There's more. This is the most important part. He asked me what your name was. I gave him your name. I used your full first name, Azarakhsh, and your last name as well. I told him who you were, just like that, when he asked."

Azi put her hand on Hector's arm and left it there. Hector did not expect to cry. It never even occurred to him that it could happen. But when he saw Azi's eyes, the tears flowed out of his as well. She moved closer and rested her head on his shoulder. After a while, she got up, went to her backpack, and came back with a crimson T-shirt.

"You can blow your nose on one side and I'll do the same on the other," she said, offering it to Hector.

When the tears had stopped, Hector said, "I'm sorry."

"There's no need to feel sorry or shame. Your life was in danger. You did what anybody would do, what I would have done, to stay alive. What we need to figure out now is what to do about this Joey, this animal."

"What we can do is stay clear of him."

"We can go to the police. We can go talk to a counselor here at school. Let's go right now. Mrs. Sherman is in her office until five, I know."

"I don't want to do that. Not yet anyway."

"Why? We're not going to let this criminal kill you."

"I'm not going to let him kill me. Azi, I decided to tell you what happened, no one else knows, because I want you to be careful. Walk away from him when you see him. Stay away from the irrigation ditch. He knows about you. That's why I told you."

"That's it? That's the only reason?"

"No . . . you're my best friend. I wanted to share this with you."

"Precisely, so we can deal with this together, help each

other, like we always do. I don't see any options other than telling the authorities about what he did and about his threats. What? Why are you smiling?"

"It's just your use of the word *authorities*. It sounded like an Iranian kind of word."

"It is. We happen to have some experience living with fear, and it's not a good way to live."

"There's one other person besides you that Joey mentioned when he attacked me: Aurora. He made it clear that if I told the authorities he would hurt her."

Azi was silent, thinking.

Hector continued. "There's a month left of school. Then we'll move to the house in Socorro, and that will be the end of living in fear. I just have to be careful until then."

Hector fell silent. He might be safer away from Joey, but what about Azi?

"I'll be all right," Azi said, reading Hector's mind. "He's not interested in me."

"He seems interested."

"Maybe in a general, hormonal way, but not specifically. And I can take care of myself."

"I was thinking that maybe . . . maybe we shouldn't be seen together."

Azi tilted her head sideways to get a better look at Hector. "Why?"

"Because he thinks you and I are . . . He knows you're important to me."

"So . . ."

"You're another way for him to get at me . . . to get into my head . . . to make me be afraid always. If he doesn't see me with you, he won't . . . I'm thinking of you . . . to protect you."

Azi was looking at him like she did not believe a single word of what he had just said. "We walk together to and from school. We go to the library together. Sometimes I come over to your apartment, and sometimes you come over to mine. And what do we do? Homework. You want to put an end to the incredible amount of time we spend together for my own protection?"

Hector could not restrain a smile. "Okay, look, there's something I didn't tell you."

"I'm listening."

"The girl that Fili is marrying . . ."

"Gloria."

"Yes, Gloria. She used to be Chavo's girlfriend. That has to be the reason that Joey is after me, and if he thinks that you and I . . ."

"Are girlfriend and boyfriend . . ."

"Then isn't it logical that he would try to do to me what Fili did to Chavo?"

"Steal his girlfriend?" Azi smiled. "You have a way of making sheer nonsense sound logical."

He touched the back of her hand. "If he says anything to you, anything, or does anything to harass you, I will go to the police. I promise."

"If he even dares to look at me the wrong way, I will kick him where it hurts."

"There you go," Hector said, thinking, *Azi would have put up more of a fight than I did.* Then he added, "Let's take it a day at a time. We won't tell anyone for now. But it's a day-by-day decision. All right?"

"All right. For now."

"I think it's almost time for your math club, and we didn't practice." Hector stood and picked up the basketball. "I'll be in the library."

"I can walk home with Rosalinda. She's in the math club. She lives near us."

"I'd kind of like to walk home with you today. It would make me feel like less of a jerk."

The way Azi looked at him—it was too late. She had already seen the jerk in him.

Azi checked her phone and said to Hector, "The competition for captain of the chess team is in half an hour. Enter the competition, Hector. I know, I know, you'll be in Socorro

High next year. So whoever comes in second will be captain. But you get to show this guy Joey that you plan to be alive next year. Show him you plan to live your life like always. His threats mean nothing to you."

Hector opened the door to the school, and Azi stepped in. After a few steps, he looked at Azi and said, "Maybe."

But he could tell by Azi's sad frown that she knew that *maybe* was his nice way of saying no. He did not wish to be captain of anything. He did not want to feed Joey's resentment. Invisibility was what he wanted and needed to survive. The hell with showing Joey any more of him than he already had.

CHAPTER 8

Hector stared, openmouthed, at the parking lot jammed with cars and at the throng of people crowding the entrance to the long building that resembled a bowling alley. Azi, sitting next to him in the last seat of the school van, raised her eyebrows and whispered, "Wow."

"All these people are here for both of you," Mr. Lozano said.

Azi and Hector walked behind Mr. Lozano and the two mothers toward the entrance. Aurora, quiet for once, held on to Azi's hand.

"I'm kind of nervous," Aurora said.

"Me too," Azi responded.

"Yeah," Hector added, his breath quickening. Azi looked and sounded a lot calmer than he felt. He heard her take a deep breath. Then, when she took another, he understood that she was showing him a way to calm down.

Hector inhaled as much air as his lungs could take and

slowly exhaled as Azi watched. "Just read it the way you wrote it," she said to him, and smiled.

Mami and Mrs. Pourmohammadi entered first. They walked tall and proud, as if they owned the place. In front of them, Hector saw a hall packed with round white tables. Each table had a place setting for a dozen people and on the center of each a miniature American flag sprouted amid a bouquet of red carnations. Toward the front of the hall, where Fili was waving at them, there was a raised concrete platform that, for some reason, was painted bright yellow so that Hector was reminded of an egg that had cracked on the floor. In the middle of the platform, there was a white lectern with a microphone next to it. The lectern, Hector immediately noticed, was not tall or wide enough to protect whoever stood behind it.

Hector decided to focus on Fili and Gloria instead. Fili looked handsome in his father's brown suit. And Gloria was . . . radiant. Her welcoming smile momentarily soothed Hector. There was no doubt that she was proud to be at the center table with the most honored guests. And the way she casually held Fili's hand conveyed to Hector that she already saw herself as a member of the Robles family. When Hector reached the table, she gave him a hug.

Mr. Lozano took charge and directed people to their places. He gave the best seats, the ones facing the speakers, to Mami and Mrs. Pourmohammadi. He put Azi and Hector next to each other facing the guests and with their backs to the stage. Hector was glad he was seated next to Azi. Maybe her serenity would rub off on him.

Mami touched the tablecloth and admired its softness. Hector stared at the place setting in front of him. He lifted one of the two forks, the smaller one, and quickly put it down. "It's for the salad," Aurora, sitting on his right, informed him. "I researched it."

"Did you tell Fili and Mami?" Hector whispered back.

"I told them to watch what I do. You might want to do the same." Then she took the napkin in front of her, waited for Fili to catch her eye, and when he did, they both placed their napkins on their laps.

"I wonder if I can order a beer," Fili said.

"Fili!" Mami and Aurora responded identically and simultaneously.

"I'm just kidding!" Fili laughed.

This was enough to set the table buzzing with conversation. Gloria was asking Mrs. Pourmohammadi to pronounce her name one more time. Mami was laughing at one of Mr. Lozano's corny jokes. Azi and Aurora were talking about a book Aurora loved. Murmurs of laughter filled the hall. It seemed as if the only one silent in the whole place was Hector. He reached for the goblet of water and drank half of it. He could feel moisture on his scalp as if the water he'd drunk had evaporated straight to the roots of his hair. There were so many people. Dozens of men and women who surely could find a better way to spend a Saturday afternoon. He had imagined something less imposing, a few old people coming together to chitchat about their illnesses and, while they were having dessert, listen to a couple of kids. But this was something else altogether. And what was most surprising was they all seemed to want to be there. The men were all in suits and skinny ties and the women had sparkling bracelets and dangling earrings and had clearly gone to the beauty shop to get their hair transformed into something more ceremonial. The whole place, these people, this event, deserved more from him than the casual read-overs he had given to his essay.

"In case you're wondering, I'm not mad or anything," Azi whispered to him.

Hector leaned closer to her. "For . . ."

"For hiding from me all week."

She'd noticed. He'd been hiding from everyone.

"Has Joey done anything . . . else?"

"He's making sure I don't forget him. You know . . . stares, hand gestures. Yesterday there was one of those gooey plastic worms dangling from one of the slits in my locker."

"I've been praying that the earth opens up and swallows him."

"That's not very holy of you."

"Have you read the psalms lately?"

"Let's not talk about Joey. This event is all the scary I need right now. I didn't expect this. I should have practiced more."

"You'll be okay. You look very . . . professional." Hector touched the sleeves of the blue jacket that Mr. Lozano had given him. Then he lifted the bottom of his brown-and-green tie. "Your father's?" Azi asked.

"Yes."

"When you go up there, just imagine that he's the only one here and you're reading to him." Azi said.

What came to Hector's mind just then was the image of his father coming home with the beautiful mahogany Mexican chess set that Hector still used at home. How old was he? Six? Seven? That same night his father taught him the rules. Where had his father, who could barely read, learned to play chess?

Hector pushed his chair back. "Excuse me," he said to Azi. "Bathroom." He walked back toward the entrance, his eyes lowered so as not to show the urgency he was feeling. To the right there was a dark hallway that looked promising. He pushed through a set of wooden swing doors and found himself in an enormous kitchen. The small cramp he'd felt at the table was tightening, twisting.

"It's this way." It was Gloria holding the doors open.

"Ahh," Hector said, grateful.

"I had to go too. I'm so glad you let me come. You look great." Gloria walked quickly with Hector following. When they reached the end of the hallway, she pointed to the right.

"Thank you," he managed to say.

"Don't worry. You'll do fine," she said.

Sitting in the blissfully quiet stall, Hector wondered about the sudden attack of nerves. It couldn't be that reading a few hundred words in front of people would cause him this much anxiety. He had read in front of people before. At Sunday Mass, he had been lay leader many times. No big deal. The only thing that he could think of was that fear had found a permanent place in his stomach ever since Joey's attack last week. Every day this past week, he had felt that unsettling queasiness in his stomach as he went from class to class, walked to and from school. His whole week had been consumed with trying to dodge Joey. Even now when he came into the bathroom, he had opened the door slowly, as if expecting Joey to be waiting for him. And it wasn't just Joey. There was also the nagging feeling that Fili and Gloria's happiness would not last. If Chavo was anything like Joey, there was no way he would let go of Gloria.

Oh, man, what's the matter with you? Don't worry, be happy. Why can't you just not be afraid that something bad is coming around the corner? The light at the end of the tunnel is not an oncoming train. Snap out of it, as Aurora would say.

The objective here was simple: Read carefully and slowly. Get through the event without any major embarrassments. He must calm himself. Go back to the table full of composure. *Try to act dignified and proud, as if Papá were here,* like Azi said.

When he finally emerged and made his way back to the table, a small bald man in a shiny gray suit was tapping on the microphone. The composure Hector had attained reading the essay one more time in the solitude of the bathroom stall vanished as the noise of the crowd quieted down. It struck him now that the essay was totally wrong for this audience. It was too personal, too revealing to share with the well-dressed, businesslike, practical-looking strangers who he saw sitting around him.

And there was more. Reading the essay in the bathroom, he realized that he was not worthy to read an essay that, in essence, described his father's courage to pursue happiness not for himself, but for his family, and the courage to face death with peace. He felt like a hypocrite—a coward who had not earned the right to talk about his father's courage.

"Hector, you all right?" Aurora leaned over and whispered loudly as soon as he was seated.

"Sure, why?" Hector placed the folded pages of his essay next to his plate.

"You're white," Aurora told him, alarmed. "Kind of yellow, actually."

Azi offered him a glass of water. Her eyes said something like *Don't worry.*

The little bald man finally got the microphone working. He introduced himself as Mr. Roark. "And the only reason I'm here's because my name has a roar in it. Roaar, get it?"

When the giggles died down, Mr. Roark proceeded to welcome everyone, but especially the first-, second-, and third-place winners and their families. Hector and Azi both looked to their right and saw a boy their age. He was wearing a spiffy, double-breasted turquoise jacket with gold buttons, gray pants, a light blue shirt, and a red tie. A very thin red tie, not like Hector's three-incher. Next to his plate was a clear plastic folder. Even from a distance, Hector could see that the boy had printed his essay using a gigantic font. Which, come to think of it, was probably not a bad idea.

Mr. Roark was standing on tiptoes so his head could clear the podium. The Lions Club was honored to sponsor the yearly essay contest, which was open to all first-year students from El Paso high schools. Over three hundred essays were submitted, and the reading committee had a very hard time choosing the best three. Everyone was in for a treat when they heard what these young people had written. And anyone who thought that patriotism or good citizenship was a thing only for old toothless lions like him (he paused to make sure people had a chance to laugh) was sorely mistaken. But first, everyone was to enjoy their dinner and have a good time.

There was a bowl with iceberg lettuce, tomatoes, and cucumbers sprinkled with a thin orange sauce. "It's French dressing," Aurora said in case anyone didn't know. She held the small fork in front of her until Fili and Hector did the same. Hector pushed a slice of cucumber to one side and stared at the lettuce. He stabbed the smallest piece and put it in his mouth. He chewed slowly. There were rumblings still going on down there, and he put his fork down. He looked up and scanned the room. No Joey. If only he could convince his bowels that there was no threat here. He tried to focus on Azi's words. She was explaining how ginger tea had reduced the swelling in her mother's ankles.

"I started drinking ginger tea after your science project," Mr. Lozano told her.

"Maybe it will help with my arthritis," Mami wondered.

The third-place boy at the next table was talking and

eating his salad at the same time. The man sitting next to him was an older, more serious version of the boy. All twelve people at that table seemed to be related. Brothers, sisters, mother, father, grandparents, and maybe an aunt and uncle, all had come to celebrate the boy's triumph. They sat and ate and laughed as if they were sitting in their dining room having dinner.

"Are you done, sir?" Hector jumped up from his seat, startled. It was a waiter who looked and sounded like Chavo.

"Yes," Hector said, swallowing. A moment later, the waiter came back with a plate. On the plate, there was a baked chicken breast, mashed potatoes with a dollop of gravy on top, and peas that rolled around.

"You're not hungry?" Azi asked.

"No." Hector touched his stomach and made a face to simulate pain.

"Did you know that for the longest time the rook was a giant two-headed bird carrying an elephant?"

"Yeah?" Hector said, grateful. She was trying to distract him. "I've seen old chess pieces of elephants with towers on their backs but never a two-headed bird carrying an elephant."

"But the bird carrying an elephant makes more sense, don't you think?"

Hector paused to think why that would be. He ventured,

"Because a rook can fly across the board? But why the elephant?"

"It's the weight and responsibility of carrying the elephant that keeps the bird from turning the wrong way."

"If you're trying to make me feel calmer, it's not working. Now my head is also in knots trying to figure out your two-headed bird!"

Azi laughed. *That* was comforting. Hector looked at her, and for once, Azi was the first to look away. A feeling of sadness filled Hector. The move to Socorro, wonderful as that was, would also mean the loss of his daily contact with Azi. Then it hit him that he was receiving the first-place award because of her and he had never read her essay, never even asked if he could read it. What kind of friend was he? All week long, he had avoided her and told himself that he was doing it to protect her. Protect her? He was protecting himself. Without Azi, maybe Joey would hate him less. The worm on his locker was an appropriate symbol. He should have brought it with him as a reminder of his true self.

There was another long trip to the bathroom, and when Hector came out, Mr. Roark was tapping the microphone and asking for silence. Hector found his seat and stared at his dessert plate, avoiding the worried looks from everyone at his table. Mrs. Pourmohammadi passed along a roll of Tums.

Next to the untouched cake, there was a cup of tea that his mother was pointing at and urging him to drink. He raised the cup to his lips and sipped.

"On a scale from one to ten, how sick do you feel?" Aurora asked.

"Nine and three-quarters."

"If you have an accident while you're up there, just head for the side door with tiny steps. No one will know." Aurora intended to be funny probably, but Hector nevertheless located the exit door and traced the path that would get him there.

Azi handed him a folded piece of paper and leaned closer to him. "I always say this when I'm afraid." Hector opened the paper and read: *The Lord is the strength of my life, of whom shall I be afraid?* "It's from Psalm 27."

Hector folded the piece of paper and placed it in his shirt pocket. He nodded thanks to Azi. Then he tried to remember the words he had just finished reading, but already they were forgotten.

Mr. Roark recited all the good deeds of the Lions Club. Hector heard the words but understood only one or two. He heard the name Robert J. Williams, and then there was applause. The boy with the turquoise blazer pushed his chair back and walked to the steps on the side of the podium. He placed the plastic folder on the lectern and opened it. Robert J.

Williams bent the microphone closer to him and scanned the crowd before beginning. He had a surprisingly deep voice that was clearly not natural, but one practiced and refined for just this occasion. Hector imagined a miniature broadcaster delivering the nightly news. He tried to understand the meaning behind the boy's words but was unable to focus for more than a few seconds at a time. Something about dreams. Tons of words about dreams. Hector's family once had a piece of the American dream. The house they lost when his father died was the dream. They had it, then the dream was gone and the nightmare in the projects began. Hector tried again to listen to Robert J. Williams. Henry Ford dreamt of a horseless carriage. The Wright brothers dreamt of a flying machine. Abraham Lincoln dreamt of a country without slavery. The boy went on listing dream after dream. John F. Kennedy, Neil Armstrong. Madame Curie. Steve Jobs. There was no end to the list of dreamers.

Hector heard the clapping and saw the boy move away from the lectern and take a small bow. He followed the boy to his seat and saw the boy's father pat him discreetly on the back. Then Mr. Roark was trying to pronounce Azi's name. What came out finally was something that sounded like Sara-Cush. Azi looked at her mother and smiled while her name was being massacred. Then she stood up slowly and floated up to the yellow stage, or so it seemed to Hector.

Azi glanced in Hector's direction, breathed, and then began. Her voice had a quiet, solemn quality to it. It reminded Hector of the times when his mother and her church friends said the rosary in the living room. Unlike the third-place boy, Azi sounded sincere. Now and then, her eyes lifted from the paper and met her mother's eyes. Her family was from Iran. Her father had been the pastor of a Christian church that met in secret. He was discovered and sent to prison, where he died a few months later. Azi and her mother escaped into Syria and then Turkey and eventually made their way to the United States. Her father wanted Azi to come to America because here she could freely live her faith, which was her happiness. Her father believed that they were made in such a way that the pursuit of our happiness would lead them to God because only God could fill their hungry hearts completely. But her father also knew that their happiness would never be complete if others were suffering, if others did not have the opportunity to seek happiness.

There was more, but Hector stopped listening because all his attention was drawn to the knot of sorrow in his chest. It wasn't just Azi's words that affected him, but her very being. He had never heard such words come from a person his age. But more than that, Azi had the kind of courage he did not have. She was proud of her father and not afraid to show it. She was not afraid to be who she was. She was the true first-place winner. The Lions either had made a huge mistake or committed an injustice. Hector heard the clapping and watched Azi walk back to her table. The clapping was not as enthusiastic as it was for the third-place boy, and this made Hector even sadder. Hector waited for her to sit down, and when she did, he said to her: "You should have gotten first place, not me."

He did not hear Azi's answer because Aurora was kicking his leg. It was his turn. Mr. Roark was looking at him. Hector stood up carefully and walked to the podium. The ball of frozen sadness in his chest was still there. He straightened the wrinkled pages as best he could and looked up to see the anxious face of his mother, Aurora's thumbs-up, and Fili's encouraging nod. He avoided looking at Azi's face because he was afraid that she would hasten the tears that were making their way to his eyes. He stared at the page in front of him but the words were fuzzy, so he opened his eyes wide and began. He read a quote by Immanuel Kant about how happiness is the fulfillment of duty and then stopped. A movement in the back of the hall pulled his eyes in that direction. There stood Joey like a churchgoer coming late to the service and waiting for the right time to find a seat. There was a silly grin on Joey's face, and his head bobbed from one side to the other. Hector looked down at his paper and tried to find the last word he'd read, but all the letters had sprung loose from the words that held them. The letters began to dance on the page. The frozen rock in his chest was dissolving and lavalike liquid burned his lungs. The words on the page got smaller, so he squinted. He managed to read the next few sentences, aware that his voice sounded weak, shaky, like thin ice about to break. The words trembled and then blurred until he could not read them anymore. He saw Joey raise his arm as if to ask a question. Hector turned sideways so that he could not see Joey through the corner of his eye. He found the exit sign on the opposite end from Joey and directed his broken speech to it.

His father came from Chiapas when the ranch where he worked was sold and then closed. His father picked lettuce in California, potatoes in Alabama, cherries in Michigan. Eventually, he brought his mother and his brother, who was two years old at the time, to the United States. Then his father got a job working at a factory in El Paso that made pants. Hector went to visit him at work one day. His father worked at a table cutting material with electric scissors that hung from the ceiling. He had to work fast. There was a daily quota he could not fall below. When he got off work, his father took a bus to a community college, where he studied to be an auto mechanic. Five years later, he got a job in the auto repair shop where he worked for the rest of his life. What his father loved most of all was working with animals and plants, but he learned to love his job as an auto mechanic. He was as good with motors as he had been with horses.

Everything inside of Hector was liquid. He noticed for the first time that there was an empty chair next to where his mother sat. That was the chair where his father would have sat if he were alive.

My father would be disappointed in me.

Hector, his words broken by small gasps, continued. After many years of work . . . Papá saved enough for a down payment, and he bought a house. It had a yard. His father planted trees and grew chili peppers, tomatoes, squash . . .

The house in Socorro is just a stupid silly dream.

His father came home from work . . . his hands cracked and black with grease. He worked on his garden in the evening. Always planted when the moon was full. He stuck his hands in the soft mud because he said the earth was healing.

All I care about is saving my hide.

So . . . what does duty . . . have to do with happiness? Happiness is what you like to do, and duty is what you need to do. But what if the duty comes from love?

Love. Did I really just say that word?

Hector knew Joey was laughing at him. And why shouldn't he? A hot, burning liquid was rising, filling Hector's eyes.

He stammered on. It took courage for his father to pursue happiness. His father's happiness was the courage to do his duty, no matter what. To support his family. It was his duty to give his family a home, and that was his happiness as well. He gave up his life every day; he even made sure to die with courage for the sake of his family's happiness.

There was a part in his essay where Hector was going to talk about his father's serenity amid the incredible pain of the last days of his life, but he didn't get to that part because water was gushing out of his eyes and nose, and from somewhere deep inside of him, he heard muffled sobs. He shut his eyes and clenched his jaw, listened to the silence in the room. Then he looked for his brother, and when he found him, Fili immediately stood and made his way toward Hector. Fili's stride was proud, defiant, as if daring anyone to laugh at or feel sorry for his brother. Hector closed his eyes and waited, his hands clenching the lectern, until he felt the strong arm of his brother around his shoulders.

CHAPTER 9

They made their way through the tables and out the side exit door, Fili holding Hector by the shoulders and almost lifting him off the floor. There was never any doubt or hesitation as to which way they should go. They were two bodies directed by a single mind. They stopped outside the door, and Fili wiped the tears on Hector's cheeks with their father's broad tie. Hector lifted the tie and looked at the stain his tears had made.

"That's all right," Fili said. "I don't think the old man would mind."

"I'm sorry," Hector said.

"Sorry for what?" Fili put his arm around Hector and held him tight against his side.

"It was like Papá was there," Hector said as they walked to the front parking lot. *And*, Hector thought, *Papá could see the coward that I am.*

"I know."

"When I wrote that essay, I didn't even think about what I

was writing. It was just words. I was trying to get a thousand words on paper and be done with it."

Fili turned Hector and faced him. "A lot of people know about Papá now. The kind of man he was. You did him proud." When they got to the truck, Fili opened the door, and Hector stepped in. "Why don't you ride back in the truck with us? I'll tell Mami and get Gloria, and we can just head home."

Hector nodded. He was glad not to have to face Joey. He had been given an opportunity to shine, and instead he had taken Mr. Lozano's famous candle and stuck it deep under a bushel of fear. What the hell was wrong with him?

"You have nothing to be ashamed of," Gloria said to him on the way home. The three of them sat in the truck's cab. Gloria was holding Hector's neatly folded coat on her lap. Hector was looking out the open window, letting the warm air sting his face. "There was not one dry eye in the place when you were up there. It was all heart, Hector. All heart."

Hector smiled. Joey was probably also moved—moved to what? To laughter? To go ahead and carry out the threat to kill him?

"Puro corazón," Gloria said, and squeezed his hand.

Hector thought about the Spanish word for heart, *corazón,*

and how similar it was to *courage*. His books on chess often spoke of playing with heart, and by that, they meant that you should play with courage. Courage was more than the willingness to take risks. It was a quality of mind that allowed a player to face imminent danger, even an inescapable trap, with self-control. Courage did not panic, did not give up. It was composure under pressure, the ability to keep the mind alert and focused no matter what. It was doing what needed to be done even when you were afraid. Courage was what Azi had shown up there on that podium reading an essay that was both deeply felt and deeply thoughtful. She had stood there in front of all, unafraid of her intelligence and willing to let her light shine in honor of her father.

Gloria chatted happily as if all that had happened was that he had been overcome with emotion. It was, in her view, a moment of sincerity that was to be treasured and valued. That kind of thing was so much better, for example, than the polished performance of Robert J. Williams, the third-place winner.

"Azi deserved first place, not me," Hector said, still looking out the window.

"I was looking at her while you were up there," Gloria said quickly, "and I tell you, Hector, you did not disappoint her in any way."

Hector reached into his shirt pocket and touched the slip of paper that Azi had given him. The Lord may have been Azi's strength, but the Lord had skipped him when it was handed out.

"Have you ever asked her out?" Gloria asked.

Hector shook his head.

"What is it with you guys? If it wasn't for us, you'd never pursue happiness. Happiness could be sitting right next to you, and you wouldn't recognize it."

"I recognized it about ten seconds after I saw you," Fili said.

Hector turned his head toward the open window and closed his eyes.

"Fili, let's tell Hector our news," he heard Gloria say. "Pull over for a second and show him."

Fili signaled with his arm that he was making a left turn, waited for an opening in traffic, and pulled into the parking lot of a church. "Well, this is a good place to pull over," Gloria joked. There was a lit sign in front of them with the name of the church and these words below:

TO BE HAPPY

MAKE SOMEONE ELSE HAPPY

Fili shifted into neutral and proceeded to dig into the pocket of his pants. There was nothing in the right pocket, so he tried the left. "Please don't tell me you lost it," Gloria said.

"It's here someplace."

"Fili!"

There was nothing in the left pocket. "I must have put it in the coat."

Gloria unfolded Fili's coat and looked. "Here it is." She pulled out a small blue box. She opened it and handed it to Hector.

Fili said, "I asked Gloria's father for his blessing, and he gave it to us. It's all I could afford right now."

"It's perfect." Gloria kissed Fili on the cheek. Then, to Hector, "I took it off before the banquet because . . ."

Hector held the ring in his hand. He could feel the happiness of Gloria and Fili, and it was not right that he should be so certain now that it would not last. *Chavo and Joey will make sure that it doesn't last.* Once again, fear began to trickle in his stomach.

"Hector, be happy for us. Don't worry," Gloria pleaded.

"I am happy for you," Hector said without conviction. He started to hand the ring to Gloria, when a car swerved from the street and stopped a few feet from the truck's front bumper.

"Oh no," Gloria said.

It was Chavo's blue Impala. Hector shielded his eyes with

his hand and saw Chavo in the driver's seat and Joey sitting next to him. Hector shouted: "Let's go, Fili! Drive away! Just back up and drive away!"

Fili turned off the ignition. Gloria was holding on to Fili's arm, shaking him as if to awaken him from the trance he had fallen into. Fili ignored her. He sat there, hands on the steering wheel, waiting, watching Chavo. "Fili, let's just go," she said.

"It's not a good idea, Fili." Hector knew his brother would not run away. Now Hector could see Joey. He was rubbing his eyes, pretending to cry.

Both Chavo and Fili opened the doors to their vehicles at the same time. Gloria held Fili back with a tight grip on his arm. Fili stared at Gloria's hand and then at her, and the intensity in his look was so strong that Gloria could not help but let go.

"I'm coming with you," Gloria said.

"No."

"Yes!" Gloria insisted. "He needs to hear it from me."

"He's heard it from you!" There was anger in Fili's voice— an anger Hector had not heard in a long time. Then, softer, "Let me talk to him, man to man. Please."

Chavo leaned on the hood and lit a cigarette. Fili walked through the space between the two cars and stood in front of Chavo, his arms loose and relaxed by his sides. Gloria moved behind the wheel so she could be closer to the open window. She clasped her hands together as if in prayer and she tilted her head so she could listen to Fili and Chavo's words, but the only sound came from the Impala's engine. Whatever Fili was saying, only Chavo heard. Hector could see Joey slumped in the front seat of the Impala as if he had fallen asleep. Hector's heart beat wildly against his chest. He noticed something inside his closed fist and realized it was the engagement ring.

The doors of the church opened, and people began to pour out in ones and twos. Hector sighed in relief. Surely, Chavo would not do anything in public. Chavo slid from the hood and moved closer to Fili. He was shorter than Fili but bulkier. He was wearing a lavender button-down shirt and black pants. Now Chavo was speaking, chest touching Fili's chest. Gloria searched in her purse and took out her cell phone. She handed it to Hector. "Call 911," she told him. She opened the door and stepped out of the truck. Hector wasn't sure of her instructions. Did she want him to call 911 now or if blows were thrown?

"Stop it! Both of you!" Gloria shouted. Chavo and Fili both turned toward her. Gloria shouted to Chavo. "You need to leave me alone! You have no right . . ."

Chavo moved away from Fili and started to make his way toward Gloria. Fili stopped him with the palm of his hand, and Chavo swatted it away. Trembling, Hector tapped the three numbers.

"911 Emergency Services—how can I help you?"

"You need to send a police car. There's an argument. My brother might be in trouble."

"Is someone hurt?"

"Not yet. But soon. Maybe. Probably."

"What is happening?"

"My brother and a drug dealer. They're about to fight."

"What's your location, please?"

Hector read the white sign. "The Church of Jesus Redeemer . . . on Lee Trevino . . ." The cell phone fell and Hector fumbled underneath the seat with his hand, but he gave up looking for it.

Gloria had made it to the driver's side of the Impala and was shouting at Chavo. A group of people stood on the steps of the church watching. A few had their phones out recording the scene. Fili had his arms around Gloria and was holding her back. He tried to push her behind him, but Gloria wriggled out of his arms and faced Chavo again. Now it was like a dance, the three of them moving in a circle. It was all happening so fast, and it was also happening as if in slow motion. Fili finally lifted Gloria off the ground and placed her away from Chavo. He walked to Chavo and pushed him back with two hands on his chest.

"It's over! Let her go!" Fili's words were loud enough for Hector to hear.

Immediately, Chavo launched at him with fists and kicks. The people in the church were shouting, and Gloria was shouting. Hector held on to the door handle. This was the time to go out and do something, but he couldn't move.

Fili covered his face, trying to block Chavo's punches. It was clear that Chavo had fought before, knew how to get around Fili's defenses. Whenever Fili lowered his arms to protect his stomach, Chavo's fists went to Fili's face. Unable to hit Chavo, Fili charged and wrapped his arms around Chavo. They fell. Fili found a way to get on top, his knees on Chavo's arms. Chavo swore curses in Spanish and in English. He spat on Fili's face. Fili squeezed Chavo's neck, and Chavo's face began to turn a brownish-purple color.

The passenger door to the Impala opened. Joey came out with an aluminum baseball bat. Hector tried to open the door handle, but his hand, his arm, nothing in his body responded to him.

"Fili!" Gloria shouted and pointed at Joey, but before Fili could turn or move out of the way, Joey stopped as if waiting for a pitch and then swung the bat. Hector saw the back of Fili's skull sink in. Fili toppled, and Chavo pushed him away. Gloria rushed to Fili's side and turned him over, sobbing.

Hector let go of the door handle and sank in the seat. He saw Gloria crying on the ground next to Fili, shaking him. Even the people in the church were now running toward Fili. He heard sirens in the distance. He saw Joey help Chavo up from the ground and saw them walk together. Joey was leading Chavo to the passenger's side of the Impala. They stopped in the space between the car and the truck. Chavo started to take off his shirt. There was blood dripping from his lips. Joey glanced at Hector and nodded with a smirk as if to indicate that, of course, Hector would choose to stay in the safety of the truck.

It was then that Hector was finally able to move. His body entered another world, one filled with a rage so old he could have drowned in it. He slid behind the steering wheel and started the truck. He found the clutch and put the truck in what he guessed was first gear. Chavo in front of him was holding the wadded T-shirt against his mouth, too stunned to understand what Hector was doing. Hector pushed the gas pedal, and the truck moved backward. Hector shifted out of reverse and tried to find any forward gear. There was a grinding sound as the gearshift finally eased into first or third, Hector didn't know which and didn't care. He lifted the clutch slowly and stepped on the gas pedal as far as it would go. Joey managed to jump out of the way before the truck lurched toward him and his brother. Hector saw the panic in Chavo's eyes before the truck exploded against his body and the Impala. Hector's chest rammed the steering wheel, and his head crashed against the windshield.

Hector felt an unexpected peace before the bright light turned to black.

CHAPTER 10

Hector opened his eyes briefly and saw a young woman with her hair pulled back putting a stethoscope on his chest. It was the first time anyone besides Azi had seen the C that Joey had written there. There was a hum inside his head. A throbbing pain in the middle of his face. He tried to stand. He wanted to go over to Fili and tell him he was sorry for not stopping Joey, but a hand pushed him down.

"Try to relax."

"My head."

"Concussion. Maybe some internal bleeding. We're taking you to University Medical Center."

Liquid seeped from somewhere in his mouth. It tasted like iron. There was pressure on his forehead. He tried to breathe through his nose. There was something stuck in there. He gagged. Coughed.

"You're going to have to breathe through your mouth. Your nose may be broken. You also have a big gash on your forehead from the windshield. You're going to need some stitches. Try to keep your eyes open."

He closed his eyes. He did not want to open them even though he knew he could if he tried. It was only with his eyes closed that he could see his father helping Fili up from the ground.

With his eyes closed, Hector could step out from the truck to reach Fili and his father. His father was on top of a white horse without a saddle, and Fili was behind him holding on to his father's shoulders. The horse was moving sideways and tossing its head up and down as if it hurt it to stand still for so long. Hector wanted to get on, but there was no room.

"I'm only taking Fili right now," his father said.

Hector looked around and saw nothing but desert and mountains in the distance. It was so bright he had to shut his eyes. "Don't leave me here!" he pleaded.

"I can't take you." The way his father said it hurt Hector. The tone was more appropriate to *I don't want to take you.*

"Why? I can change. Papá, please! I can be brave like Fili."

Fili touched the back of his head and then looked at his bloodied hand.

"I'm sorry, Fili." For a moment, Hector thought of telling Fili that the door to the truck got stuck as it sometimes did. But there was something about the place where they all were that made Hector feel as if only the truth could be spoken. "I was scared. I was afraid and just sat there. I'm so sorry."

"That's all right," Fili said, and there was understanding and forgiveness in his voice. "Don't let being scared ever stop you from helping."

"I won't. Not anymore. But take me with you. What will I do here?"

There was a smile on Fili's face. It said to Hector, *That's for you to figure out.*

Hector tried his father. "I want to come with you." The horse began to move. "Please, Papá!"

"Not yet," his father said. "You're not ready. It's not balanced yet. We have to go now."

"Papá, don't leave me here. It's not safe for me. I'm scared."

"You got things left to do. Do them." His father's voice was firm but kind.

Fili stretched his hand as if to touch Hector or wish him peace. Hector saw the horse turn at the corner.

"Come back!" Hector shouted after them. "I don't want to be here!"

He was on a high bed partially enclosed by a blue curtain. To his right, a window let in a ray of sunlight. He reached up to touch the pain on his head. There was a bandage on his forehead, and he couldn't breathe through his nose. A woman was standing next to him.

"Your face shattered the windshield. You have a bad con-cussion. They'll do some tests later to make sure there's no brain damage." The woman was old, tired-looking. She wore a wrinkled black dress with white dots the size of golf balls. Hector turned away from her and reached for his nose. There was something hard and tight in each nostril.

"Cotton plugs. They'll take them out later today. A small fracture, but your nose is as straight as ever."

"My brother?" He asked the question even though he already knew the answer.

"I'm sorry. He didn't make it. He passed last night. A few hours after he got here."

Hector shut his eyes. He felt the touch of the woman's hand on his arm. There should have been tears. There were tears back then when Joey carved his chest. There were tears at the banquet. There were no tears now. He was glad. He didn't want tears. He felt hard inside. He felt hard and sharp like an ax, and that was good.

"I took your mother and your sister home early this morn-ing. Your mother was not doing very well. They asked me to call them when you woke up." The woman reached for the purse behind her, on a chair.

"Don't call her." Then, in a somewhat softer tone, "Yet." Let his mother rest. He needed time to think. That dream or vision that he had. What did it mean? He needed time to figure out his father's words: *You're not ready. It's not balanced yet.*

"Okay." The woman closed her purse. Hector saw a white cloud floating softly across a blue sky. The woman was still there moving her lips, as if searching for the best words. "My name is Mrs. Encina; I'm a social worker here at the hospital. I'm also a lawyer, but I'm talking to you today as a social worker, okay?" The cloud moved on. Hector waited for other clouds to drift into view, but none came. "You're in a secure unit of the hospital. An ambulance brought you here yesterday afternoon. The police turned you over to the custody of the Juvenile Probation Department. In a few minutes, a probation officer will interview you to determine whether to formally charge you with delinquency. The police collected statements from many witnesses who saw you drive the truck into Ignacio Mendez. Ignacio is in serious condition downstairs. He has two broken legs and a smashed-up pelvis and possibly some internal bleeding, but he'll live. He's going to be in a wheelchair for a long while."

Fili is dead and Chavo is alive.

"Hector, please listen, this is important. What you did, if it was intentional, is the equivalent of a felony in the adult world. It's very serious. If the probation officer determines to initiate a petition for delinquency, you'll be taken to juvenile court as soon as you are released from here. There you will be arraigned before a district judge who handles juvenile cases and then sent to the detention center until a court can adjudicate your case. Henry Flores, the probation officer who is going to talk to you, is a good man and a friend of mine. He's letting me talk to you first. What you say to him is very important. Maybe we can avoid the formal process. I've been talking all night to your mother and your sister, so I know a little bit about you. You are a good kid. A good student. No prior problems with the law. When it comes to juveniles, no one wants to make a bad situation worse. It's all about rehabilitation and not about punishment."

Hector didn't answer. He understood only a few words of all that she said. Smashed pelvis. Wheelchair. Delinquency. Some words he had no clue as to their meaning. *Arraigned. Adjudicate.* His brother was dead because he didn't act. He's the one that should be dead, not Fili.

I'm only taking Fili right now.

"Hector, what we are looking at here, depending on what you say, is that Officer Flores can decide to put you on some kind of probation. Maybe you do community service while you continue to go to school and live at home. That would be the best outcome."

The truck had lunged forward with incredible force, but

Joey had jumped out of the way. The last thing he remembered seeing was Chavo putting out his right arm, palm forward.

"The reason I wanted to talk to you before your interview with Officer Flores is that . . . I talked to your sister and she said that you don't know how to drive a stick shift . . . or any other kind of car for that matter. She said that, a few times, your brother took the two of you to the church parking lot to practice. That you could never find the right gear. So, given what she said, I'm thinking that you were looking for reverse and accidentally put it in first. That you ran over Chavo by accident. If that's what happened, then there's no crime involved."

Now puffy white clouds moved slowly one after the other, like floats in a parade. Those kind of cumulus clouds, he remembered their name, are rare in El Paso. They are made by the evaporation of large bodies of water. But El Paso is in the middle of the desert.

Those clouds were like Joey floating in front of him with a baseball bat. And he just sat there, watching.

"Hector, do you understand what I am saying to you?" She tapped his hand. "This is your life we're talking about. Were you putting the truck in reverse?" Mrs. Encina waited. "Some of the witnesses, people from the church, they said they saw the truck go back, stop, and then go forward. You put it in reverse. The truck stalled. You tried again, but this time you accidentally went forward. Think about it. Do you understand why I'm asking you this?"

The curtain opened, and Hector heard a man's voice. "It's time, Esther."

"Two more minutes, Henry, please."

"Come on, Esther. You're gonna get me in trouble. SOP, I'm supposed to get first crack at a statement. You can stay and listen if you want."

Hector did not look at the man who was speaking. He was seeing the back of Fili's head and then the aluminum bat making contact.

Crack. Or was it more like a *twang*?

"Give me one more minute? Okay, Henry? I'll owe you."

"One minute." Henry Flores walked slowly out of the room.

During Easter, Aurora made cascarones. The only three colors she used to paint the empty eggshells were violet, pink, and blue. They were sad-looking things. Hector cracked them on her head when she wasn't looking. Hours later, she would still have bits of confetti stuck in her hair.

"So, what do you think, Hector? Was it possible that you missed reverse, that it was an accident?"

Hector remembered the smirk on Joey's face when Joey saw him frozen with fear in the cabin of the truck. What did Fili say to him in the dream?

Don't let being scared stop you from helping.

Helping who? He turned to look at Mrs. Encina and said, "If I was looking for reverse, that means I was running away."

Mrs. Encina reflected on Hector's words, nodded cautiously. Hector saw that she was as old as his mother. A tiny woman with dangling coral earrings that stretched her earlobes. "There's nothing wrong with that. Your life was in danger. You had just seen your brother get hit with a bat. You were next. Getting away was the smart thing to do."

But there *was* something wrong with that. It wasn't the truth. It was a lie. It's what a coward would do. He was sick of being a coward. His father and Fili were disappointed in him. They didn't come out and say so in the dream, but he could feel it.

"I don't know," Hector said quietly.

"What don't you know?"

"I don't know exactly what happened. I need to think."

She lowered her voice. "Hector, there's not much to think about here."

"Yes, there is."

Mrs. Encina sighed. An old woman's sigh. Like the sound his mother made when she stepped out of the bedroom where his father fought for air. Mrs. Encina moved so that her body blocked Hector's view of the window. "What happened yesterday was a tragedy. A series of rash mistakes.

Maybe you made one of them. The loss of your brother and the sorrow that you and your mother and sister will now have to go through is enough to atone for anything you might be punishing yourself for. And you'll find other ways to make up for whatever mistakes you think you made. There's no need to make it worse by landing yourself in the system." Mrs. Encina stopped. Hector thought that maybe she was thinking about all the kids she knew who had been placed in the system. She took a deep breath and continued. "I've been talking to your mother and your sister for half the night. You don't belong in the system."

He'd meant to drive forward. It was the one unequivocal, full-hearted decision he'd made in maybe all his life. That was the truth. But the truth meant prison, being sent away from his mother and Aurora. They had just lost one son. They didn't deserve to lose another one.

"What about Joey?" Hector asked.

"Joey? José Mendez? Chavo's brother?"

"Where's he?"

"The police took him to the juvenile detention center last night. He tested positive for heroin. Apparently, he smokes the stuff. He didn't have much in his system, but it was enough for him to claim that he didn't know what he was doing. Says he thought his brother was getting strangled and just lost it. He's still going to be charged with something. He's being arraigned this morning. The probation department decided to initiate formal proceedings against him. He claims he blanked when he saw his brother getting choked."

Joey killed his brother, and the old woman in front of him was asking him to go back to his life as if nothing happened. *It's not balanced yet.* That's what his father meant. The score wasn't even. It was as if Joey had taken his knight and he had only taken one of Joey's pawns. There was a choice to be made between his mother and Aurora and a life of continued fear, or finding the guts to even things out. But not yet. If thinking was what he did best, then he was going to think carefully about what needed to be done.

"I am not sure what happened," Hector repeated.

A sad, tired smile appeared on Mrs. Encina's face. "Okay, Hector. Look, when Henry comes in, tell him your mind is foggy. You need time for it to clear. You do have a concussion, after all. Give yourself a break here."

Hector thought for a few moments. He nodded. He could say that. It wasn't the exact truth, but it was close enough.

CHAPTER 11

The nurse informed him that he had two visitors. Hector figured it was his mother and Aurora. Was he up to seeing them? Not really. Seeing them was bound to sway the choice he had to make: revenge, or his mother and Aurora. Hector told himself to be strong and not let that happen. He needed time.

"Okay," Hector said to the nurse.

Aurora opened the curtain and rushed to his bedside. She grabbed Hector's free hand, and all his defenses just about melted. "Okay. I'm okay," he said. His hand still in hers. He waited until she finished drying her tears with a corner of his sheet. "Where's Mamá?"

"She wanted to come, but I convinced her to stay home. She's hurting. Her friends from church are with her."

"Who did you come with?" The nurse told him he had two visitors.

"Azi and me took the bus. She's outside. She wanted me to come in first."

Hector felt his heart beat fast. He had prepared himself for his mother and Aurora, but Azi was another matter. How could he protect the decision he needed to make from Azi? If anyone could see through him, it was Azi.

Hector pushed a button next to him, and the bed sank down. He had raised it as far as it would go so he could look out the window. Aurora sat on the chair next to his bed, and now he was almost even with her. Her face looked like she had been crying nonstop and on the verge of continuing. It was difficult for Hector to look at her. He stared at the ceiling.

"You look awful!" Aurora pointed at his forehead first and then his nose. He had not looked in a mirror but could feel the sixteen stitches that ran down from the top of his head to his eyebrows, and the bump on his nose.

"People have been coming to the house all day. Mr. Lozano. A boy from the chess team. He said he was captain of the chess team. I don't remember his name. Azi and her mother have been with us all the time. Can I bring her in now?"

Hector opened his eyes and shook his head. "No." He said it with more force than he meant to. "Not now." He touched his face, as if he did not want Azi to see his broken condition.

"She won't care what you look like." Then, "She didn't before."

Hector almost smiled. The toughness he was trying to

grow inside of him didn't stand a chance with Aurora and much less with Azi.

Hector rubbed his forehead. "What's Mamá going to do . . . with Fili?"

"The church ladies are taking care of almost everything." There was a long pause. "He'll be buried next to Papá."

A man about Fili's age came in and put a tray on a movable table.

"Manny's paying for the funeral," Aurora went on when he had left. "He said Fili had life insurance of five thousand dollars."

Hector felt a pang of shame and worry. What would happen to Aurora and his mother if he wasn't there to help? He closed his eyes.

"You know what Mrs. Encina said?" Aurora continued, excited. "She told us that she was going to file an awful death lawsuit against Joey. She's done some investigating and thinks Chavo, being that he's Joey's guardian, can pay. Maybe she can get us enough to buy the house in Socorro."

"*Wrongful* death," Hector said, tightening his jaws so as to quash a smile. Just then, he wanted with all his heart to reach out and hug Aurora. "Not 'awful death.'"

"It was both. Awful and wrongful. But don't tell anyone, because she doesn't want Chavo hiding his money."

"I won't."

Aurora crossed her arms. It was a gesture that Hector recognized. That's what she did whenever she wanted to keep herself from crying. "Can I bring Azi in now?"

Hector sighed. He turned his head toward the window. Then, after a long while, he nodded.

"I'll be outside getting a soda."

"Aurora," Hector said before she stepped out of the room. "I'll be all right. I need some time."

Aurora came back to Hector's bed and offered him her fist to bump.

A few minutes later, Azi came in. She held her backpack in her left hand and a handful of daisies in the other. She was wearing the flowered dress she liked to wear to church. Her black hair was held back with two barrettes in the shape of orange butterflies. Even from a distance, Hector could tell that she'd been crying. Hector braced himself.

"You look horrible," Azi said. She placed the flowers on the bedside table and sat on one of the plastic chairs.

"Aurora said you would be used to that."

"Your little sister is pretty smart."

"Yeah."

"How do you feel?"

Hector made a gesture with his hands. What could he say?

Azi said, "I'm sorry . . . about Fili."

Hector bit his lip, and tightened his jaw. Azi reached out for his hand, but he moved it back before she could touch him.

"I hope you're not blaming yourself for his death. You are, aren't you? I know you, Hector."

"Then you must know I'm a coward."

"No, I don't know that. Why do you say that? If you had stepped out of the truck, you'd be dead too. Fili's death is not your fault. If anything, it's my fault."

"Yours?"

"Think about it. If I hadn't bugged you to write that essay and then conspired with Aurora to send it, you would have never gone to the banquet—"

"Okay, I get it."

"It sounds stupid, doesn't it? All of the *if I had done this or done that* is silly thinking."

"If I had jumped out of the truck and done something to stop Joey, Fili would be alive. That's not silly thinking."

"Okay, I understand the guilt you're feeling now. It's normal. But don't let the guilt make you throw your life away."

Hector fixed his eyes on hers. "Why do you say that?"

"Mrs. Encina said you didn't want to say you were looking for reverse."

"Maybe I wasn't."

After a few moments of silence, Azi continued. "This morning, the man from the juvenile probation department came to talk to your mother. He talked mainly to me because your mother can barely concentrate. He said he talked to you already. He's putting together a report for the judge. Family situation, school history, that kind of thing. He knew a lot about you already. He had talked to Mr. Lozano. He knew about the Lions Club award and even about how good you are at chess."

"It doesn't matter."

"What do you mean it doesn't matter? Hector, look at me!" Hector slowly moved his head toward Azi. "It does too matter. You don't belong in the same place they're going to send Joey."

"Maybe I do."

"You can't think that way. Mrs. Encina said that you can get out of this with just probation. She's got everyone you know writing letters about how smart and what a good kid you are. Mr. Lozano, your boss at the supermarket. There's no point in sending you away. You're not like Joey and Chavo. I hate those guys! If they ever stood in front of something I was driving, I would crush them like bugs!" Azi waited for Hector to say something. When she saw that he wasn't going to, she said, "Please, Hector. You need to choose life right now. You have to say to yourself: *Whatever my faults or mistakes, it is my duty to choose life.*"

"Pursue happiness."

"Yes! It is your duty, like it was for your father."

"Fili was pursuing happiness."

"Oh, Hector. You're—"

"A genius. I know."

"That wasn't what I was going to say . . . not this time."

Hector watched Azi's face. She was not only smarter than him but wiser. But she didn't know him, not really. She didn't know what it was like to watch your brother get killed while you sat there doing nothing. How could he live with himself knowing he had let his brother die? Azi didn't know how angry he was deep down at Fili for choosing Gloria over his family. Azi didn't know about Elbereth, his secret fantasy. He could go on and on. How could he pursue a happiness he did not deserve? Didn't he have to do something about the disgust he felt for himself first? He smiled at her and stretched out his hand for her to hold. "Thank you, but . . ."

"Don't, Hector. Don't do this to yourself." Azi's eyes filled with tears.

"I need to be alone now. Please."

A look of resignation crossed Azi's face. She had said all that could be said. Hector reassured her with a smile.

"Okay." Azi stood slowly. She came over to the side of the bed, took Hector's hand, and placed it on her cheek. "Remember the scripture verse I gave you at the banquet?"

"The Lord is the strength of my life, of whom shall I be afraid?" Hector waited for Azi's smile and then he watched her leave the room.

But where the hell was the Lord and his strength when he was afraid?

CHAPTER 12

Hector was sitting with Mrs. Encina outside the courtroom of District Court Judge Lisa Galvan when Joey and a man in a gray suit walked past and entered the courtroom. Joey did not look at Hector when he walked by. There was a subdued, almost sleepy expression on Joey's face, one Hector had never seen before. His face was pale and drawn as if all blood had been drained from it. Hector could see Joey's right hand tremble.

When the door of the courtroom closed, Mrs. Encina said, "I heard the boy's been in detox. He started showing withdrawal symptoms at the juvenile center. Did you know he was addicted to heroin?"

"No." Hector's mind went back to the Piggly Wiggly parking lot. He recalled the slight slur when Joey spoke, the floating eyes, the cinnamon breath.

"His lawyer will no doubt use that in his defense."

Hector remembered the focused way Joey walked toward

his brother, the powerful swing of the bat, the smirk when he stood in front of the truck. "He knew what he was doing."

Mrs. Encina turned sideways to look at Hector as if trying to understand him. Finally, she said, "Your family is worried about you. They say something's the matter with you. I have to say, you don't seem like you give a damn about your future. These past few days you've hardly spoken to Aurora or to your mother."

"What's there to say?"

"The doctor who treated you told me you might have some form of PTSD. You know what that is?"

"Post-traumatic stress disorder."

"Correct. It makes sense after what you've gone through. I'm going to make sure you get the help you need to get past this. But today you need to talk to the judge. No more of this macho stuff, this silence. The judge needs to know that you'll be okay living at home. The only way she will know that is if you talk. What you did back there in that church parking lot was not the real Hector. You are a kind, thoughtful person. A good student. That's the person you need to show the judge."

"Okay." But showing the judge that side of himself was a lie, at least a partial lie. There were more parts to him, and the other parts weren't so pretty. What would he say to the judge? Would he lie and say he was trying to find reverse?

All the thinking that he had done in the hospital and the day he spent at home had gotten him exactly nowhere. He was still torn between lying and going home to be with his mother and Aurora and Azi or telling the truth and then trying to find a way to balance things. Hector did not know exactly how the balancing was to be accomplished, but he knew it started with the truth. Lying would be a continuation of being his old coward self. He would tell the truth and then find a way to make Joey pay for what he did.

Half an hour later, Henry Flores, the probation officer from the hospital, opened the doors to the courtroom and said to Mrs. Encina, "You're on."

"Hold on," Mrs. Encina said, standing up quickly. "What did the judge give the Mendez boy?"

"She hasn't decided yet," Officer Flores said. Then, just as they were going in, "You didn't hear it from me, but her clerk told me she called a reformatory school in San Antonio during a five-minute break. If I were a betting man, I'd say Mendez is traveling."

"San Antonio? For how long?" Mrs. Encina asked.

Henry Flores lifted his index finger to his lips and held the door open.

Mrs. Encina whispered to Hector, "Show the judge that you do not deserve to be locked up."

The courtroom was so bright with overhead fluorescent lights that Hector had to blink a few times and wait for his eyes to adjust. Everything seemed white. The walls and the ceiling, the blinds on the windows. The only color in the room came from the red-white-and-blue of the flag and the black robe of the judge sitting high up front and waiting for Hector and Mrs. Encina. Joey and the man in the gray suit were sitting behind one of two tables in front of the judge. Henry Flores motioned for Mrs. Encina and Hector to sit next to him on the other table.

"I'll be with you in one minute," Judge Galvan said. She put on a pair of glasses and began to read from a brown folder. The judge was younger than Hector expected. For a moment, he thought she looked like an older version of Azi. She read the way Azi did in class, with both hands over her ears in total concentration.

The judge took her glasses off and nodded to a man below her to the right. He raised his hands and held them poised over a machine that looked like a small typewriter. "Good to see you, Esther," the judge said to Mrs. Encina.

"Good morning, Your Honor."

"Are you here as a social worker or as a lawyer?" Judge Galvan asked with a smile.

"As a social worker, Your Honor. I understood that the

probation department was recommending probation. I didn't think Hector needed a lawyer."

"Relax, Esther. Mr. Robles is well protected with you at his side."

"Thank you, Your Honor."

Judge Galvan looked at Hector and then at Joey. "Mr. Robles, would you be kind enough to look at me?" Hector raised his eyes. His heart was pounding.

Judge Galvan waited for Hector's eyes to meet hers before she spoke. "Mr. Robles, what was your brother doing when José Mendez hit him?"

Hector spoke slowly, trying to give himself time to think. "They were on the ground. My brother was on top of Chavo." Hector began to cough. Mrs. Encina poured water from a beige pitcher into a glass and offered it to Hector. Hector drank and put the glass on the table.

"Where were your brother's hands?" Judge Galvan asked.

"My brother's hands were on Chavo's throat." Hector turned to see Joey's lawyer smile.

"Do you think your brother was strangling Chavo?"

"Your Honor." Mrs. Encina stood. "Maybe I should put my lawyer's hat back on. What does this questioning have to do with Hector?"

Judge Galvan smiled. "Relax, Esther. This is not a trial.

I just want to determine Mr. Robles's state of mind." When Mrs. Encina had sat down, Judge Galvan said, "Do you want me to repeat the question, Mr. Robles?"

"No. I remember it. I have no way of knowing whether my brother was strangling Chavo or just holding him down. That's my brother's state of mind, not mine."

Judge raised her eyes as if she were impressed. "Fair enough. Tell me what happened next."

"Joey came out of the car. He had a bat in his hand. He walked over to where my brother was. Joey gripped the base of the bat with two hands. He took aim and swung. He hit my brother on the back of the head as hard as he could."

"Your Honor . . ." Joey's lawyer stood, but Judge Galvan motioned for him to sit.

"And where were you at this time?" Judge Galvan asked Hector.

"I was in the truck."

"Just watching?"

"Calling 911. But yes, *just watching*, as you say." Hector couldn't keep the anger out of his voice. Mrs. Encina tugged discreetly at his pants.

"Tell me what happened next."

"Joey helped his brother up, and they walked back to the car. My brother's truck and Chavo's car were parked hood to hood about six feet from each other. Joey and Chavo stopped in front of the cars."

"Go on."

Hector took a deep breath. This was the moment all that thinking had been leading up to. Right then and there he had to decide whether to stay at home with his mother and Aurora or follow Joey and do what needed to be done to balance things out. He turned his head in the direction of Joey. He saw him swinging the bat against his brother's head, saw him carving a C on his chest, saw him at the Lions banquet, raising his hand, witnessing his tears. He felt unbearable hate inside of him, and the hate was a force too hard to resist. If he told the truth, maybe the judge would send him to San Antonio as well.

"Mr. Robles, please look at me. What happened next?"

Hector fixed his eyes on Judge Galvan. "I scooted over on the seat until I was behind the wheel. I started the truck. I tried to find first gear but got reverse instead. Then I tried again and found first or third gear, I'm not sure. I stepped on the gas."

"You stepped on the gas? You wanted to go forward? Deliberately."

"Yes. I wanted to go forward."

Mrs. Encina stood. "Can I speak to Hector, please?"

"Why? Mr. Robles is telling us the truth. Aren't you, Mr. Robles?"

"Yes."

"I appreciate your honesty, Mr. Robles. One last question. What was going through your mind when you stepped on the gas?"

Hector lowered his head in thought. Then he spoke softly. "I'm not sure there was anything going through my mind at that moment. There was . . . anger, pain."

Judge Galvan nodded as if she were familiar with those states of mind. "Thank you. You may sit down."

Silence filled the courtroom. Mrs. Encina tapped Hector's hand. She looked defeated. Judge Galvan rested her chin on the palm of her right hand for a few minutes and then spoke.

"It seems to me that there is only a difference in degree between what Mr. Mendez did and what Mr. Robles did. As far as I am concerned, both of you committed similar delinquencies. Mr. Mendez says he saw his brother getting strangled, and he was acting to save him. So, Mr. Mendez, to save your brother, you grab a bat and hit his assailant on the head? You couldn't have tackled Mr. Robles's brother? Kicked him even? Hit him in the arms with the bat if you must. But to hit the head with an aluminum bat with the force that you did indicates more than a desire to save your brother. From where I sit, I believe you intended to kill Filiberto Robles. I don't care how addled your brain was with heroin fumes. You had sufficient intention to do harm."

The man in the gray suit stood up, started to speak. "Your Honor—"

"Not now, Mr. Oliver. I'm speaking to Mr. Robles and to Mr. Mendez." Judge Galvan glared at Joey's lawyer.

"I'm sorry, Your Honor."

Then Judge Galvan turned to Hector. "And you, Hector Robles. Apparently, you are a good person, a good student. I've read all the letters from your teachers. An excellent chess player, et cetera. Yet, from where I sit, I believe that when you stepped on that gas pedal, you intended to kill Ignacio Mendez or José Mendez or both."

Hector felt the blood rise to his face.

"It seems to me, Mr. Robles, that of the two of you, your actions are the most offensive. José over there, all he knows is violence. He grew up with violence. His mind was stupefied with drugs. He reacted the only way he knew how. But you, Mr. Robles, you can think. You grew up in a good family. You have the ability to act differently."

There was total silence. Judge Galvan took a sip from a glass of water. She seemed genuinely angry. But when she next spoke, her voice was softer.

"I think that I could send both of you to one of my colleagues down the hall so you could be tried as adults. Or I can send both of you to a detention center until you're eighteen and after that to adult prison for another ten years. And maybe I will do that. I don't know. Mr. Mendez, I am going to divert your case. I'm going to put off making a final decision for six months."

Judge Galvan turned toward Hector and exhaled loudly. "Mr. Robles, the Juvenile Probation Department and the DA's office have not initiated a delinquency proceeding in your case. They recommend probation with residency at home, anger management classes, community service. I'm sorry to say that this time I don't agree with their recommendation." Judge Galvan looked at Henry Flores briefly, then fixed her eyes first on Hector and then on Joey. "I want both of you to attend Furman Academy in San Antonio. In six months, I will review your behavior and go from there. I want to warn both of you that it's not going to be enough to stay out of trouble for six months. Furman Academy is not a prison. It is a school with academic classes and programs. I want to see a committed and wholehearted participation on your part. Do what Furman asks you to do and do it with enthusiasm. Oh, and by the way—one of the things that I will take into consideration six months from now is how you two behave toward each other. There will be no hostility of any kind between the two of you. You so much as look at each other the wrong way, I will send both of you—I don't care who starts it—to an adult prison. I strongly advise finding a way to get rid of the hate. I'm talking to both of you." Judge Galvan stared first at

Joey and then at Hector. "Okay, that's all. We'll resume with the next case in fifteen minutes."

Judge Galvan stood, and everyone stood. Hector saw her leave through a door in the back of the room, her black robe flowing behind her.

Mrs. Encina slammed her purse onto the table. "What the hell just happened?"

She took the phone out of her purse and started typing. Then Hector noticed Joey. He was looking at Hector with a dumb look on his face, as if surprised that he and Hector had received the same punishment.

What Joey saw on Hector's face was a wink and a grin. The fear was still there, but for once he wasn't showing it. It wasn't fear of Joey this time. It was fear of the path he had just chosen. The opportunity had presented itself, and he had chosen to balance things out.

He was going to kill Joey.

CHAPTER 13

Hector was sitting on the curb outside his apartment at 5:45 a.m. He had a small cardboard suitcase next to him, the same one his mother had brought from Mexico when she'd come to join his father. On top of that was a paper bag with the burritos his mother had made. The night before, he had promised her and Aurora that he would wake them up at 5:30 so that they could have breakfast together, but instead he had tiptoed out of his room without waking them. He wrote a note on the back of a telephone bill: *Don't worry about me. I love you.*

At 6:01, a brown sheriff's car turned onto his street. The car slowed as it approached. Joey was in the back seat. Hector had thought about the ride with Joey and had prepared himself over the past three days. Two of those days he'd spent at University Medical Center getting tested for brain damage and evaluated for PTSD by a psychologist. The brain scans showed his brain to be undamaged, and he put on a good show for the psychologist. It was hard to hide the seething anger or his new life's purpose of revenge, but he needed to make sure that the psychologist would not deem him mentally unfit to go to Furman with Joey. What was impossible to hide was the grief he felt for Fili. He walked around expecting to hear the rattle of the old truck coming down the street, but the sound never came.

The last day with Aurora and his mother was the toughest. They'd tried hard, but they could not conceal the pain of losing Fili and now losing him. Hector saw on his mother's face the still-raw sorrow of Fili's death, and Hector knew he was responsible for it and would soon be adding a lot more.

Hector stayed in his room as much as he could, letting the presence of Fili's things transform his grief into the anger he would need for however long it took to carry out his plan. He had time. He didn't have to kill Joey the first day or even the first week. So long as Joey and he were in the same place, he could wait. The thing to do was to watch Joey and determine what type of opponent he was going to be. If Joey was still set on killing *him*, he would make his move sooner.

Just as the car stopped in front of Hector, Aurora came out of their apartment. She ran toward Hector in her pink pajamas and hugged him. Hector dropped the suitcase on the sidewalk and put his arms around her. They did not say anything. One of the officers stepped out and turned Hector around. Hector placed his palms on the roof of the car as the officer patted him down. Then the officer placed Hector's suitcase inside the open trunk. Hector did not look at Aurora's face as he stepped into the car and closed the door. He placed the palm of his hand on the window as the car made a U-turn. Aurora gave him a thumbs-up through her tears.

They pulled out of the projects onto Zaragoza Road, heading toward I-10. The two officers talked briefly about previous trips to San Antonio. Hector looked at Joey and waited for him to look back, but Joey seemed oblivious to the world. Joey took off his sweatshirt, balled it up, put it between his head and the window, and closed his eyes. There was a foul odor coming from his breath, his pores, or both. They were on the highway for only a few minutes when Hector heard Joey snore.

Hector studied him. The kid had muscles bulging out of his T-shirt. A tattoo of a snake, fangs dripping poison, covered most of his forearm. There were dark bristles on Joey's cheek and chin. The wide forehead and soft eyelashes gave him an intelligent look that was missing when he was awake. Joey slept with his mouth wide open. Here was someone who could kill another human being and sleep like a baby. Hector had slept maybe a total of six hours in the past week. Hector would have killed him right then if he'd had a knife. He would have stabbed him in the heart ten times before the officers knew what was happening.

Just then, as if sensing Hector's thoughts, the officer on the passenger side turned to look first at Hector's hands and then at Joey. "Damn! That kid smells."

"It's the detox. Poison comes out of you every which way," responded the officer driving.

"Thought the kid was clean by now."

"He's clean enough. That school he's going to wouldn't take him if he wasn't."

"Clean enough still stinks. Man! I'm opening the window. The hell with the heat." Then to Hector, "You guys going to room together?"

"I don't know," Hector said.

"Get some nose plugs—and earplugs—if you do."

Hector watched Joey gasp for air. He was familiar with the struggle to breathe, the sounds the throat and nose made when they hungered for air. One time, when he'd been home alone with his father, he'd heard Papá struggle for air. He'd gone into his parents' bedroom and seen the oxygen mask on the floor. He was putting it back on Papá's face when his father stopped him.

"Thank you, Son," his father whispered. "I needed . . . to see if it was time. It's hard to know . . . with the mask."

Hector looked at Joey. Where did the kind of courage that his father had possessed come from? Was it something that you were born with? Hector hoped there were other ways of getting it, because he was going to need it.

About three and a half hours into the trip, the officers stopped for gas and coffee at a town called Fort Stockton. Hector went to the bathroom, and when he came back, the officer who had been driving was shaking Joey awake.

"You better go pee because after this we're not stopping until we get to San Antonio." Joey had a blank look on his face as if he had no idea where he was. "That way!" The officer pointed to the side of the gas station.

The second officer came out with a plastic bag and a cardboard tray with two coffees. "Lunch," he said, rattling the bag.

"It's not even ten," said the other.

"Must be lunchtime somewhere."

The two officers and Hector sat in the car, windows open, waiting for Joey.

After five minutes, the officer behind the steering wheel said, "Think he ran away? You better go check."

"Run away? Where? In this town? I think this place is worse than where he's going." The officer opened the passenger door and reluctantly walked to the side of the building. He came back alone a few minutes later. He leaned into the passenger window. "The kid's having problems."

"What kind of problems?"

"The kind you don't want to talk about before eating."

"Buy him a large coffee. Black."

"I got him one of those sports drinks and some tacos."

"No good. Caffeine. It's the only thing that works."

The officer outside went back into the store.

Hector noticed a paper bag on the side of the car where Joey had been sitting. There was a small picture frame, facedown, on top of a pair of blue jeans. Joey had brought a picture with him. Maybe it was a picture of Joey and Chavo. Hector thought of turning the frame over but decided against it. He knew all he needed to know about Joey.

Joey entered the car and tucked the paper bag under his legs. Hector looked at the two officers. They had walked to a picnic table on a grassy area away from the gas station. One of them was smoking a cigarette. The other one was on his phone. Hector ignored the fear in the pit of his stomach and forced himself to speak. "You know I'm going to kill you, don't you?"

Joey finished wiping his mouth with the back of his hand. He chuckled. "Stop pretending you're a badass. I saw you trying to be one in the courtroom. You're just a coward. Always will be."

"Cowards can kill."

Joey was closing and opening his mouth as if trying to figure out what he was tasting, oblivious to Hector's words. "I need to eat something. What you got in here?" Joey opened the bag with Hector's lunch. He took out a burrito wrapped in tinfoil and brought it up to his nose. "Chorizo! Bean or egg?" He began to unwrap it, dropping the tinfoil on the floor of the car. Hector's blood began to boil. He could reach over now, strangle him., but one look at Joey's arms and he knew that Joey would overpower him. And there was something empty and unsatisfying about killing someone who was not afraid of you, someone who thought you were nothing but a weakling. He had to make Joey feel frightened, powerless, humiliated—the kind of things he was feeling.

Joey said, his mouth full, "Good! Un poquito más salsa, ¿qué no?"

"You don't believe me?" Hector tried to keep his voice steady. "I *will* kill you. Maybe not now. Next week. Next month. You be thinking about it. First I'm going to own you." *He's not laughing*, Hector thought. *He knows I mean it.*

Joey scrutinized Hector, as if trying to remember where he had heard those words before. "Yeah, let me eat."

Hector seized the half-eaten burrito out of Joey's hand and threw it out his window. "You don't get to eat my mother's food." Hector's voice quivered with anger.

Joey muttered, his mouth still full, "I shoulda just taken that bat and done you too."

Hector saw one of the officers throw the cigarette on the ground, stomp on it. He said to Joey, "You know what I realized in the courtroom when I saw you making all kinds of excuses for killing my brother? *'I thought he was getting strangled. I wasn't thinking straight on account of the dope.'* I realized that deep down you're nothing but a gutless liar."

Joey grabbed Hector's forearm and squeezed. "You the one with the C, ¿qué no? Who stayed hiding in the truck?"

Hector shook his arm free, looked at the marks that Joey's fingernails had made. "That guy's gone. Poof. No más." It wasn't true. The frantic beating of his heart was there to remind him that he was still the same old Hector. But at that moment, Hector knew he had to remake himself.

Joey grinned, as if genuinely amused by Hector's words, like he was listening to a child say he was going to fly someday. One of the officers opened the door to the car. Both Hector's and Joey's faces must have been flushed with angry blood, because he said, "You two trying to kill each other already?"

It was Joey who responded, calmly, "Man, I could use a smoke. How about it? I need it bad, man."

The officer ignored Joey, got in, and started the car. He honked for his partner to get off the phone. Finally, he turned around and handed Hector and Joey each a cup of coffee. "Have some caffeine. It's the only drug you're getting for a long, long time."

Furman Academy was waiting.

CHAPTER 14

Furman was situated on an old air force base and that's what the place looked like. A tall kid who introduced himself as Jerry took Joey and Hector around what he called the "campus" while they waited for Colonel Taylor to get out of a staff meeting. Hector saw the barracks where kids lived, or dorms, as they were called. They were long aluminum sheds that had once housed the airmen. Classes were held in a two-story cinder-block building that used to be the base's administrative head-quarters. The gym was a converted airplane hangar.

"It's electrified," Jerry said to Joey, who was studying the chain-link fence. "See those three wires up on the top? It's almost impossible to climb over the fence without touching them. The last kid who tried ended up in the infirmary unconscious. When they took his clothes off, his balls were the size and color of ripe avocados."

Joey stared up at Jerry, wondering whether to believe him.

"I kid you not," Jerry said without even the hint of a smile.

"Besides, no one tries to escape. Where you end up if you get caught is a hell of a lot worse than here. Most everyone here knows that for a fact. Let's go back inside and see if the colonel is ready to see you."

They sat next to each other on wobbly wooden chairs. Joey was holding the paper bag with all his things on his lap. Hector had his suitcase. In front of them sat a woman typing on a keyboard. She was big and looked mean. The woman got up, went to a printer, retrieved two sheets of paper, and went back to her chair. She did not look at them once. They could have been part of the dingy furniture for all she cared.

Jerry came in and stood in front of the woman, waiting for her to look up.

"What?" she said impatiently.

"They're all set. I got Mendez in D-20 with Pina. Robles is with Dominguez in D-12. Got them sheets, towel, the usual package."

"When I first started working here, we used to de-lice, shower, and deodorize a kid as soon as he got here. I miss those days." The woman gave Joey a quick glance.

"They'll each get a haircut before their heads hit the pillow." Jerry ran a hand over his crew cut.

"The head's not the only place lice live," the woman said.

"I can't help you there," Jerry responded, laughing.

"Tell Antonini to make sure these two shower." There

was another look at Joey. Hector repeated the room numbers to himself and did the math: *We'll be eight rooms apart. Perfect.* A red light blinked on a telephone console, and the woman picked up the phone. She listened and hung up. "José Mendez, you're up."

Joey stood slowly, then bent down for his bag.

"Leave it there," the woman said. "We need to search it."

Joey stopped to consider the woman's command. They locked stares. The woman won. She walked to a door on the opposite side of the room, opened it, and stood by as Joey disappeared into a dark space. Then the woman came back and stood in front of Hector for a second, as if waiting or hoping that Hector would give her attitude. Hector didn't.

Jerry walked over and asked silently for Hector's suitcase. He took it along with Joey's paper bag to an empty table and began to go through each. After a while, he came back, handed Hector's suitcase to him, and placed Joey's bag in the chair where he had been sitting. "You won't need most of the stuff you brought. You could have traveled light like your buddy." Jerry glanced at Joey's bag.

"He's not my buddy."

Jerry was about to reply, when they heard shouting coming from the room Joey had entered. The shouts were not Joey's.

"Haven't heard him yell like that for a while," the woman

said to Jerry. "Your friend must have really pissed the colonel off." She seemed happy, finally.

"He's not my friend," Hector said. *What is it with these people?*

There was no more shouting. But now and then the woman would look at her watch and she and Jerry would exchange glances, as if something unusual was happening. There was nothing for Hector to do except imagine how he too would be yelled at. He practiced looking straight ahead, letting the shouts roll over him. Then, at one point, he happened to look at Joey's bag on the chair next to him. The picture frame was on top, right-side up this time. It was a black-and-white picture of a woman with two small boys by her side. Chavo, about twelve years old, came up to the woman's shoulder. Joey, holding the woman's hand, was maybe three. Joey had a cowboy outfit: a felt hat tied with a string around his chin, boots, holster with a silver pistol. He even had a tin sheriff's star on his chest. *The only person smiling was the woman, the mother,* Hector thought. She was wearing a white dress with embroidery around the sleeves. The kind of dress Indigenous women wore in parts of Mexico. Hector reached over and turned the picture over. He did not know why, but it bothered him that Joey once had a mother. It interfered with the image of the evil monster who smashed his brother's head.

The door to Colonel Taylor's office opened, and Joey

walked out, eyes blinking and pale, as if he had just stepped out of a four-month hibernation. He stood listless outside the open door until Jerry came up to him. "Grab your stuff—I'll take you to your room." Joey walked past Hector and took his bag. It was the first time that Hector had seen him rattled.

"You're up, Robles," the woman said.

Colonel Taylor's impeccably neat office, complete with American flag, added to Hector's impression that he was entering a prison. On the dark-paneled walls Hector saw pictures of men dressed in jumpsuits, white aviator helmets dangling by their side, standing in front of fighter jets. Hector stood in front of a cheap-looking steel desk. The colonel, sitting on a plain wooden chair, wrote in a tiny notebook. When he finished writing, he stuck first the notebook and then the pen in his shirt pocket. Next he opened a manila folder and read quietly for a few minutes. Hector wondered what he should do with his arms. He stuck his hands inside his pockets and took them out. Without moving his head, he saw a card table. There was a chessboard on the table with a match in progress. Hector studied the positions of the chess pieces. The match was being played by inexperienced players. There was no visible order or strategy behind their moves.

When Hector looked in front of him again, he met Colonel Taylor's cold stare. "You're the chess player," Colonel Taylor said. There didn't seem to be a question mark at the end of that sentence, so Hector didn't answer. He looked at his feet because he found it uncomfortable to look at Colonel Taylor's eyes. Colonel Taylor stood, went over to the chessboard, and walked over to Hector and leaned on the desk. Even in that crouched position, the man seemed imposing. He was one of those slim men who seemed to be all muscle and long bones. Hector couldn't tell whether he was bald or had shaved his head. The man was uncomfortably close. Hector gathered that his discomfort was precisely what the man sought. Hector got ready for the shouting to start. Nothing. When Hector looked at him, the colonel lifted his eyebrows ever so slightly, as if to say, *I'm still waiting.*

"I used to play chess," Hector finally said.

"And yet, here you are," Colonel Taylor said after another long pause.

Hector couldn't help but smile.

"What's so funny?"

"Nothing."

"Nothing, *sir*," Colonel Taylor corrected him.

"Nothing, *sir*," Hector parroted.

Now it was Colonel Taylor's turn to smile. He straightened up, went to the chair behind the desk, sat down. Hector was grateful for the additional space. He breathed out, fully, for the first time since he'd walked into Colonel Taylor's office.

Now comes the shouting, Hector thought. Only Colonel

Taylor didn't look like a man who was about to shout. What, then? Silence?

Hector did his best to return his steady gaze, trying not to blink first, but in the end, he had to look away. After the ten-hour drive, he was too exhausted to play this kind of game.

A few moments later, Colonel Taylor pushed a button on his phone.

The speaker crackled. "Yes?" Hector recognized the voice of the dour lady in the front office.

"What's Robles's room assignment?"

"Jerry's got him and the Mendez boy going to D. Robles to D-12 with Dominguez and Mendez to D-20 with Pina."

Colonel Taylor reflected. "Put Robles with Alberto in D. Put Mendez in C."

"Jerry already left with Mendez."

"Call him on his walkie-talkie."

"The only room vacant in C is C-18? That means Mendez will be in a single."

Colonel Taylor reflected, glanced at Hector. "That's all right. We'll move someone in there soon."

"Also, Alberto's not going to like getting a roommate. He worked hard to get a single."

"He'll live."

"All right, if you say so."

"One more thing, Lucy."

"Yesss?"

"Any empty seats on the van that's going to the U tomorrow?" The colonel looked briefly in Hector's direction.

"Let me check." Hector could hear a drawer open, papers shuffling. "Two seats."

"Put Robles on the list."

There was silence.

Wouldn't it be easier to just open the damn door and talk to each other?

"What about the other kid? Mendez?"

"No, just Robles. Thank you, Lucy."

There was a loud click on the speaker. Colonel Taylor pushed a white button and then looked up at Hector. The eyebrows were raised again as if asking Hector if he had anything to say.

Hector wanted to ask what the U was and why he was being sent there but not Joey. But that would make it seem like he cared, and he did not. During the long trip here, after he threw the burrito out the window, he had decided that a new Hector would be the one setting foot in Furman. Why not? No one knew who he was. He could pretend to be a badass, like Joey said, and no one would know not to believe him, if the acting job was good enough. The scar on his forehead didn't hurt.

"Okay, Hector."

"Okay?" Hector didn't understand.

"You can go. Wait for Jerry. He'll show you to your dorm."

"That's it?"

Colonel Taylor chuckled. "What would you like me to say to you? Whatever I can say to you, you already know, or you'll figure out pretty soon. You'll either be one of our best students or the worst. It's up to you."

Hector sat there wondering what kind of mental game Colonel Taylor was playing with him. He suddenly wanted to convince the man that he would be the best student. Being the best was easy for the old Hector. But the new Hector was going to kill José Mendez and that would probably make him the worst student Furman ever had.

Hector nodded to signal that he understood the choice. He stood, turned around, and walked out.

That choice, the choice between good and bad, had already been made.

CHAPTER 15

Jerry waited for Hector to get his suitcase, and then they walked outside. Kids were coming out of a side door with books in their hands. They all wore the same gray pants and white T-shirts or button-down short-sleeved shirts. The same buzz haircuts on all of them. If it wasn't for the varied color of their skin, or for the acne in a few of their faces, they'd have all looked like the same person reflected in a hundred mirrors.

"What's the story with you and Mendez?" Jerry asked. It was hard for Hector to keep up with the boy's long strides. Jerry slowed down but did not wait for Hector to answer. "I had the two of you in dorm D, but the colonel wanted you in separate dorms. Are you in rival gangs or something? You don't look like a gangbanger."

"He killed my brother and I almost killed his," Hector said. He was tired of thinking about what to say and what not to say. What difference did it make what people knew?

"Both of you lucked out when you were sent here," Jerry

said. "Everyone at Furman could've ended up in a worse place. Did the colonel tell you about the three-strikes-you're-out policy?"

"No."

"It's what it sounds like. You mess up three times and you're out of Furman. An RA or a teacher can give you a demerit. Three and it's *adeeos, amigo*."

What about killing someone?

"Except fighting," Jerry added. "One fight and you're out."

"Even if you don't start it?"

"Look," Jerry said, as if cutting to the chase, "if you want to have it out with your buddy Mendez, there are two legit ways of doing it. You two can bang each other at the boxing ring or you can play basketball against him. Almost anything goes on the basketball court."

"Boxing ring?" Hector asked, intrigued.

"Talk to Sansón, your roommate. He'll tell you what to do to set up a GM."

"GM?"

"Grudge match."

Hector looked at Jerry. He seemed to be about Fili's age. A scar on his cheek indicated some kind of violent former life. Jerry caught Hector's gaze. "You work here?"

"Yep. I'm an RA. Resident assistant. Most of the RAs here were once Furman students. Some of us went to college and came back. Others decided to stay after they graduated from Furman."

Hector chuckled.

"What? You find it hard to believe that people would choose to come back?"

"You say 'graduated' and call kids here 'students.' This isn't a school, it's a prison."

"Clearly you have never been in prison. You might change your mind after tomorrow. The colonel's got you going to the U."

"The U?"

"U as in the University. That's what we call the federal prison that some students are *asked* to visit. I've never seen anyone get put on the list an hour after they got here. What did you say to the colonel?"

"I barely spoke."

Hector had heard of visits to prison, had seen TV documentaries about it. Prisoners shouting at delinquent kids, showing them where they are headed, scaring them into good behavior. But why hadn't Joey been sent? There were two seats in the van.

They stopped at one end of dorm D, a long corrugated steel structure with rows of windows on each side. Hector supposed that there were only two entrances to the building. The one they were about to enter and a similar one at the opposite end of the building. Hector saw two similar buildings on each side of dorm D. He figured that the building to his right was dorm C, where Joey would be staying. Just then a set of steel doors opened, and a group of kids, all in gray shorts and white T-shirts, streamed out. One of them began to bounce a basketball as soon as he was out.

"You reffing today, Jerry?" the boy with the basketball asked.

"I'll be there in a while." Jerry caught Hector examining the steel doors. "The doors to the dorms are never locked because of fire department regulations. But an alarm is set at lights-out, and if you open the doors, you'll wake up half of San Antonio."

They walked through a dark hall with rooms on each side. Except for the first room, the rest had no doors. Hector peeked through the openings to each room as they walked by. Each was identical: two beds, a lower and an upper bunk, two desks, two chairs, and two dressers. The showers and toilets were in the middle of the dorm. The toilet stalls had a half door and the showers had curtains. Otherwise, Furman did not seem to be big on privacy. But no doors on the rooms also meant that he would have easy access to Joey when the time came.

Jerry stopped in front of a doorway and pointed. "This is your room." Jerry went in and peered at a cork bulletin board in front of one of the desks. "Looks like Sansón is on work detail. He'll be back soon." Jerry patted a bundle of linen on the top bunk. "Sheet, pillowcase, towel, blanket, which you won't need." Then he touched a blue bag. "Toiletries and all the clothes you'll need in here. Antonini is your RA. His room is by the entrance. He'll cut your hair and get you your schedule of classes. I'll tell him you're all set for tomorrow. Be outside the colonel's office at eight a.m. Any questions?"

"No."

"All right." Jerry stepped out of the room and then came back. "Oh, one more thing. Sansón earned the right to have a single room, and now he's being asked to give it up. Try to be grateful, if you can find it in you."

Before Hector could respond, Jerry had done an about-face and was gone.

Hector was feeling dizzy, slightly claustrophobic, hot. There was one window in the room, but it was only open a crack. It did not seem possible for two persons to live in such a small space at the same time. Hector picked up his suitcase and placed it on top of the empty desk at the other end of the room. He imagined his mother on the train from Chiapas carrying the same suitcase all the way to Juárez, where his father was waiting for her. Hector touched the suitcase as if it were his mother's hand. He remembered Aurora's word-less hug in front of their apartment. For a moment, he felt like crying. Instead, he shouted an obscenity at the top of his lungs. The new Hector didn't cry. He opened the suitcase and began to take out its contents and put them in the small dresser next to the desk. He stopped when he got to the plastic bag with his mother's rosary and three twenty-dollar bills. Sixty dollars was equivalent to a week's worth of groceries. He put the plastic bag in the front drawer of his desk. He tore a page from one of the notebooks on his roommate's desk. He found a pencil tied by a string to the bulletin board and wrote down Joey's room number. He put a pillowcase on a pillow that looked like it had died and someone had forgotten to bury it. He tucked the piece of paper inside the pillowcase.

C-18. That's why he was in this miserable place. That's what he had to remember.

CHAPTER 16

The following morning, Hector and eight Furman students waited for the van to arrive. They sat on wooden benches outside the main entrance to Furman. Hector kept touching the top of his head and then looking at his palm. The evening before, Antonini had clipped his hair off with what looked like an instrument from the Middle Ages. It was a crab-like mechanism that yanked out a chunk of hair every time Antonini squeezed the handles. Hector touched his head when the scalping was complete, and there was blood on his fingers. But Hector liked the haircut, if you could call it that. It gave him a delinquent look, like all the other Furman students.

A student with a blue cap was mowing the lawn on a tractor. Hector admired the skill with which he maneuvered around trees and trucks. A beaten-up white school van pulled up the driveway. Everyone sitting on the benches stood at once.

Hector was at the end of the line waiting to go on board when someone tapped him on the shoulder. It was Sansón, his roomate. Sansón was appropriately named; he was massive. He reminded Hector of an ancient Toltec statute. When Hector had seen him come in to their dorm room the day before, the room had become even smaller.

"Hello, Hector!"

Hector's eyes widened. The impression that Hector had of Sansón was that he looked like a violent criminal on the outside but was a harmless child on the inside.

"You going too?" was all Hector could think of saying.

"I sign up every time. If there's room, they let me go. I checked this morning, and there was an empty seat."

"Why?"

Sansón hesitated. He shuffled his feet, embarrassed. "My father's there. They let me visit with him."

Hector and Sansón sat behind the driver. Hector waited for Sansón to make small talk, but Sansón was silent, and for that Hector was grateful. Among the many things that had kept Hector up half the night was the mystery of why Colonel Taylor had placed him in the same room with Sansón. Was Sansón, like this prison trip, supposed to keep him from avenging his brother's death? Was that the strategy that the colonel had come up with after reading his file?

Two kids in the last seat of the van were comparing past experiences in juvenile detention centers. They joked and boasted about who had been in the worst place. But after an hour or so, the conversations stopped. They turned off the main highway and traveled down a road that became more desolate with every passing mile. Run-down houses with mangy dogs and the remains of gutted cars in their front yards turned into shabby house trailers rusting permanently on cement blocks. Even these disappeared before the rose-colored complex came into view.

A wire fence with rolled razor wire on top kept Hector from getting a good look at row after row of identical buildings. The place was a sinister version of the projects back home. The prison consisted of a series of one-story, flat structures that looked as if they had been lowered into place by a helicopter one piece at a time. The only height came from the three flagpoles and the floodlights that shot up into the sky every twenty yards. The only evidence that human beings dwelled there was a deserted basketball court.

The driver of their van, an old man the students called Yoda because, Hector guessed, of his pointed, hairy ears, went to what looked like a side entrance. A giant section of the fence miraculously slid open when the bus pulled up to it. Everyone on the van turned around to see the fence close and bolt shut behind them. Then they waited, trapped between two rows of fence, until a guard wearing a black baseball cap approached and told them where to park. The students filed out of the bus and followed the same guard through a small entrance and into a brightly lit room. There they sat on cheap plastic chairs that must have been white at one time but were now a dirty beige. The room seemed to be designed for prisoners, not visitors. There were no windows, and the two doors looked as if they were forever shut. Hector saw in the faces of the other students the same claustrophobia he was feeling. Hector thought he had prepared himself for ugliness, but this was wasn't ugly. Ugliness at least had life. This here was sanitized death. The place smelled of the liquid used to preserve the dissected frogs in his science class. The only sound came from the hum of neon lights. It was so quiet that Hector could hear Sansón's breath next to him. They were not even inside the cells and already Hector could feel his stomach twist and shrivel.

"This place gets to me every single time. I'll never get used to it," Sansón said quietly. Hector knew that Sansón was wondering how his father could survive in such a place.

Finally, a woman dressed in a dark skirt and white shirt told them, in a robotic voice, what to expect. "You have entered a minimum-security prison." Hector looked at Sansón as if to say, *If this is minimum, what's maximum like?* "You have special permission to visit the cell of your host inmate. In order to ensure the safety of those proceeding beyond the visitors' lounge, all the inmates have been remanded to their cells for the duration of the visit, which is to last no longer than one hour. Because of you, the inmates had to give up their outside time. Consequently, some of them are unhappy. Under no circumstances are you to engage in conversation with or respond to in any way to anyone other than the inmate you have been assigned to or a guard. And one more thing—a piece of personal advice." She seemed to finally come alive here. "Take a good look around, because this, or worse, is where some of you might end up."

They followed her single file down a hallway into a big locker room with wooden benches. Hector could see urinals and curtainless shower stalls through a side opening. The woman told them to strip down to their underwear and socks and put on the blue jumpsuits in front of them, then left to give them some privacy. Five minutes later, she returned to lead them through another hallway to a red iron door. The woman signaled at a camera and waited for the door to be opened from the inside.

They entered a waiting area that resembled a hospital operating room except this room had dozens of stainless-steel tables and chrome stools bolted to the white floor. The room was a circle surrounded by gray doors. Each door had a small glass window the size of a shoebox, and Hector could see men's faces peering out of them.

Five minutes later, the red door opened and nine convicts in orange jumpsuits entered the room. The inmates formed a straight line in front of the students. The woman guard spoke, her voice now impatient and angry. "When I call out your name, come to the front and stand in front of the inmate with the hand raised." The guard began to read the names of the students from a sheet of paper in front of her, and the students began to line up in front of their inmates. Sansón went to the biggest, widest man in the room—clearly his father. Every student's name was called except Hector's. Inmates, students, and the woman guard went out a door, and Hector was left alone. He looked around the room and saw the eyes looking at him through the windows on the doors. The room was some kind of common area, and maybe the doors would open and the faces behind those windows would come out. Had the woman guard made a mistake and forgotten to read his name?

Hector tried to swallow, but he could not find a single drop of saliva. He looked at his feet, trying to avoid the faces peering through the glass slats in the door. He could hear shouting coming from the cells. Shouting directed at him. Isolated words reached him: *kid, like, hands, nice, soft, hard, baby. Suck.* Then some of the prisoners began to bang on the doors, and the shouting increased so much that Hector could no longer make out any specific words.

He sat on a stool trying to think of something, anything other than where he was and the possibility that the doors would open. It was all part of the scare tactics so that he could see where he was going to end up. He had prepared himself for being scared, had imagined people shouting in his face, but this was terrifying. The catcalls behind the doors, the sense of time stopping, was oppressively real. No matter how much Hector knew that the whole point was to frighten him, what he felt now was physical. There was not enough air to breathe, and the little that made it to his lungs was like scalding water. Hector remembered the fear that filled him at the Lions banquet, the trips to the bathroom. How would he compare that fear to this? There was no comparison. That fear was imaginary. Even Joey's threats created a different kind of fear. The difference was the aloneness that he felt at that moment. There were hundreds of people behind those doors but he was alone. More than alone, forsaken. And also this: With Joey it was the present that was frightening. Here it was the present *and* the future. If he killed Joey, he would be sent to a place like this or maybe worse.

A lifetime later, or so it seemed, the red door opened and an old-looking inmate came in. He had long gray hair that looked like it had never been washed, but the top of his head was bald. He was thin, with tight, wrinkled, and tattoed skin barely covering his bones. The guard that accompanied the inmate also seemed older than the woman guard. The two of them stood side by side comfortably together like old friends who didn't feel the need to talk anymore. The guard motioned to Hector. Hector followed the two of them. Corridors turned into other corridors. If inmate and guard were suddenly to disappear, Hector would not be able to find his way back to the common area. Years later they might find his dry bones. Finally, the old guard stopped in front of one of the cell doors. There was a number and a name on the side. CORTINA—01333. The inmate motioned for Hector to enter first. The guard left the door to the cell slightly ajar.

Hector saw a single bunk covered tightly with a faded gray blanket, a combination stainless-steel sink and toilet, a bookcase, a chair, and a desk. The bookcase was completely filled, and there were books stacked high in piles on the floor, making it almost impossible to walk. On the desk there was a paperback, a stack of legal folders, two sandwiches of unusually white bread, and a banged-up tin pitcher filled with a dark liquid. The walls of the cell were bare except for a poster of a Buddha with rays of blue light shining behind him.

"Hector Robles, right?" the inmate said, lifting books from the chair and placing them on the desk.

"Yes."

"Cortina," the man said, pointing at the chair.

Cortina waited for Hector to sit and then sat on the bed. He filled the glasses with a dark liquid from the pitcher and handed one to Hector. Hector took the glass and drank. It was some kind of powdered drink that was supposed to taste like cherry but ended up tasting like a combination of chalk and bleach. Cortina took one of the sandwiches and offered the other to Hector. Hector declined. The bologna or whatever it was that stuck from the sides of the bread looked pale and sickly.

"Go ahead and take a bite," Cortina said. "Might as well get the full experience." Hector could see that inmate was not going to remove the plate from his face until he grabbed the sandwich. He placed the glass on the desk and lifted the sandwich from the plate. He took a small bite of sandwich. There was no mayonnaise or mustard on it. It must have been a good three minutes before Hector had chewed enough to be able to swallow the chunk of cardboard-like food in his mouth. There was a grin on the skeleton-looking face of Cortina. Apparently he was amused by Hector's effort to get the stuff down his esophagus. Hector took the plate from his lap and placed it next to him on the desk.

"So, what do you think so far?" Cortina asked.

"It could be worse," Hector said, trying to sound nonchalant. His heart had not stopped banging against his chest.

"Yeah, that's true," the inmate answered with a smirk, as if that was the kind of smart-ass response he had expected. He looked around the cell. "I've lived in this little hole for fourteen years. And you're right, it could be worse."

Hector stared at the toilet briefly. That single bite of bread and dead meat was doing something to his stomach.

Cortina said, "Coming here was a reward for the twenty-two years of good behavior in what you would call a worse place. This here is what I worked for. It's quite luxurious, as you can see. And not having a cellmate is a highly unusual privilege. This day and age."

Hector tried to detect irony in Cortina's words, but the man was apparently being sincere. There was a rumbling in his abdomen, and Hector moved to the edge of the chair. He wrung his hands. "I need to use the toilet."

"So use it," Cortina said without moving.

Hector hesitated. Then, embarrassed, "It's number two." He crossed and uncrossed his legs.

"Number two?" Cortina said, faking shock. Then, still not moving, he said, "It's funny. When I first got to prison, I thought crapping in front of my cellmate was one of the worst punishments of prison life. How humiliating! Having someone watch you, listen to your bodily noises, smell the digested outcome of food."

"Please, I need to go."

"Then go."

"Could you step outside?"

Cortina laughed—a short, mean laugh. "What are you going to do when you're here? You'll have to do twenty-two years of good behavior like I did before you get a private cell. In the meantime, are you going to ask your cellmate to step outside?" Hector and Cortina looked at each other. There was no give in the man's eyes.

Hector crouched his way to the toilet at the end of the cell. He fumbled with the snap buttons of the jumpsuit until he found a way out and he dropped on the cold steel of the toilet. He covered his eyes with his hand for privacy. When he looked up, he saw that Cortina was poring over a book. When he was done, Hector put himself back together and gingerly returned to the chair.

Cortina closed the book and fixed his eyes on Hector. "You have any questions about prison life?"

"What did you do? That got you in prison?"

Cortina ignored the question. Instead, he said, "The colonel left a message for me. He said he was sending me a smart one. Is that right, Hector? You got brains?"

"I have brains," Hector said.

"Well then, you'll love it here. The quiet. The time to think, read. Look at all those books." Cortina turned in the direction of the stack of books on the floor. "Of course, it might take you a while to get these kind of accommodations. Private room with your own bathroom. So, Hector with brains, what do you like to do?"

"Do?"

"What gets your rocks off? I mean, besides the satisfaction you get from thinking of yourself as smart?"

Hector was stung by the insult. Or was it just an observation? Still, Hector felt a pressure to respond. "I like chess."

"A chess player!" Cortina said, full of mock admiration. Then, still looking at Hector, he said, a serious tone now, "I was twenty-five and the young man I killed was twenty-three. I was sent to death row. This is Texas, after all. But after ten years, my sentence was commuted to a life sentence without parole."

"You have to spend the rest of your life in prison?" Hector said, surprised.

"No," Cortina said firmly. "I'm not a prisoner. I got out of prison back when I was still on death row." Cortina waited for Hector to understand. Then, seeing that Hector didn't, he said, "Hate and fear are the real prison."

Hector nodded.

"As for this"—Cortina looked around—"yeah, I'll be here for the rest of my life with any luck. But who knows? I half expect some bureacrat in the Texas Department of Criminal Justice to figure I have it too cushy here and maybe send me back to maximum security. Could be I'll run into you there."

Hector waited to see if the words were said with humor. They weren't.

Cortina went on. "I didn't kill that man out of anger—

although I don't think I ever hated anyone as much as I hated that man. I executed him. In the few seconds that passed between the time I decided to kill him and the time I pulled the trigger, there was nothing but cold, naked hate."

Hector's words came out of him before he could stop them. "What happened to the hate?"

Cortina smiled, as if finally Hector had said something that mattered. "It's still there." Cortina paused. Hector could see this was a painful subject for the man. But Cortina continued. "Whenever I think about what the man did and why I killed him, hate returns. But I no longer do its bidding."

It was not the answer Hector was expecting. He thought his hate was like a hunger. It would go away after he fed it Joey. But Cortina was right—how could he ever forget what Joey did?

"The man I killed"—Cortina's voice was shaky—"took someone very precious from me. It took me a long time to understand that it's a lot easier to hate than it is to mourn."

Hector did not understand. The best way to mourn Fili was to avenge his death. He blurted out, "I don't want to be a coward."

"Good luck with that," Cortina said matter-of-factly. "We're all cowards. Every one of us, one way or another." Cortina lowered his head in thought. "I've watched my own cowardice with my mind's flashlight for many years. Looking at it doesn't make it go away. It just helps me live with it. As far as I can tell, that's what courage is, finding a way to live with our cowardice."

"The mind's flashlight?"

"Yeah," Cortina said. "Look up my buddy Díaz when you get back to your school. He's one of the teachers there. He'll fill you in on the flashlight."

There was a knock on the door. The old guard poked his head in the room and said, "It's time."

Hector stood. He waited for Cortina to offer his hand or say something, but Cortina was already looking for his book. Just as he was stepping out, Cortina said, "Hey, Hector, you want to know the first step to living with courage?"

Hector shrugged. "Sure."

"Give up on revenge."

Hector stared at Cortina, perplexed. He shook his head that he did not understand.

"It doesn't make sense right at this moment. But one day it might. Now go, class is over. You're welcome." Cortina began to read.

The drive back to Furman was like riding inside a hearse. The only sounds were everyone's deep breaths. Hector was sure everyone was thinking the same thing: *I*

don't want to end up there. Then there were those mysterious words that Cortina had spoken. *Courage is finding a way to live with cowardice. Give up on revenge.* The words sounded profound, but Cortina was right—they made no sense. If you found a way to live with cowardice, weren't you a coward? If you gave up on revenge, you were letting fear rule you—fear of confrontation, fear of the consequences. Hector grabbed the side of his head. There was too much stuff going on in there.

"Makes you think, don't it?" Sansón asked Hector.

"Yeah," Hector answered curtly. He wasn't in any kind of mood for talking.

Sansón continued. "I've been there maybe eight times, and every time I come out, my head hurts with thinking. Guess that's why they call it the U!" Sansón laughed, and Yoda the driver turned quickly and glared at him. Apparently, laughter was not appropriate after a visit to the U.

Hector exhaled. "Yeah."

"It hurts to see my father locked up and me not helping out with the bills at home."

"How long are you at Furman?" Hector asked reluctantly.

"The judge gave me a year. I did two months at a juvie place, and then Colonel Taylor got me into Furman."

"What'd you do to get a year?"

"I liked beating up kids."

Hector looked at him long and hard. He couldn't imagine Sansón hurting anyone.

"When I get outta here, I gotta be able to read. I can get a better job if I can read. How can I be an auto mechanic if I can't read the manuals or work on computers?"

It came to Hector that Sansón was just like Fili. It wasn't just that they were both into cars. What Gloria say about Fili? That he had a purity and innocence about him. The description applied to Sansón as well. Fili was dead. Joey killed him. That's what he had to keep in mind. Yes, the prison trip just added another layer of fear to his resolve for revenge, but he owed it to Fili to not give up. How could he give up on revenge? Things needed to be balanced. It wasn't just revenge. It was justice he was seeking. And how could he possibly stop hating? Even Cortina admitted that wasn't possible. No prison trip was going to stop him. Then Hector remembered something Jerry had said on the way to the dorm. "You're a boxer?" he asked Sansón.

"I did some amateur boxing before I got into trouble."

An idea came to Hector just then. He spoke impulsively, without thinking. "Jerry said to talk to you about setting up a grudge match."

"Oh, not me. X-Man does that. I just ref the fights sometimes."

"I can teach you how to read better if you teach me how to box."

"Really, ese? You mean it? Yeah, man. Deal."

The look of childish joy on Sansón's face made Hector wish he could take back his offer. Teaching Sansón to read was going to be some kind of torture. And how much boxing could this clumsy monster teach him? He was on the losing end of a very bad deal.

Hector leaned on the window and closed his eyes. No more talking. No more thinking. It was time to act.

CHAPTER 17

Three days later, at 6:15 a.m., Hector was running with fifty other kids around the school's soccer field. His head felt strangely cold without his hair even though sweat poured out of every single pore of his body. He looked up to the front of the pack and saw Joey in the lead. Sansón was the only student behind Hector. Sansón weighed a good one hundred pounds more than he did, but was not breathing hard or showing any signs that he was struggling. Instead, there was a pleasant smile on his face, as if he were going slow on purpose, to save Hector from the embarrassment of being last.

"Five more laps. Pick it up," Antonini, the murderous barber, yelled from the middle of the pack.

Hector began to increase his speed. These morning runs, which inevitably turned into races, were good opportunities to humiliate Joey. He planned to catch up to Joey, insult him, and then outrun him. It would show Joey and others that he was not afraid. It would also prove to himself that he could overcome his own fear and act as if he had courage. Insulting Joey, outrunning him, embarrassing him, were small steps toward the ultimate goal of "owning" Joey before he killed him.

Hector was counting on Joey's heroin-ravaged lungs to give up on him. He figured Joey would run out of gas after the first lap, but Joey was still going strong while Hector's legs were beginning to feel like wet noodles. Sitting for hours trying to conquer Maestro I did not exactly prepare him to run twelve laps first thing in the morning. Still, Hector planned to use the mental concentration that he used in chess to ignore the burning lungs and the other assorted pains he was feeling. He went by the group of kids in the middle of the pack who were simply jogging to complete the mandatory three-mile run. It was the half dozen who were half a lap ahead of everyone who, incredibly, were running as if there were some kind of reward for first place. But what could serve as a reward in this place? Maybe the winner could skip the most boring classes Hector had ever sat through. What the hell was Joey doing in the front?

With two laps left, Joey finally began to fall behind. Hector sped up. He caught up to Joey when there was one lap to go, but the effort to get there was so great that there was not sufficient air in his lungs for speaking. The best Hector could do was flip Joey the middle finger and then, with all the might remaining in his body, push past. Joey's face turned red for a few moments before taking up the challenge, just as Hector had hoped. By the time they entered the last hundred yards, the two of them were running side by side with visible anger. Some of the kids behind them were shouting, "Go, Topo, go!" and it came to Hector that Topo was Joey's Furman name and that the crowd was cheering for him. The cheers filled Hector with rage, and rage brought energy.

"You're nothing but a piece of mierda. A brainless, useless piece of mierda," Hector said to Joey, and then began to move past. Joey increased speed as well. Hector saw the finish line a few yards ahead of him. He was about to raise his fist triumphantly when he felt two hands grab and then pull down the back of his shorts and underwear. Hector stumbled to the ground, his behind bared for all to see. A laughing, mocking Joey stood over him and then walked across the finish line. Hector tried to stand up and fell again. By the time he pulled himself together, Joey was surrounded by a group of students who were cracking jokes at Hector's expense.

"Man, I thought it was morning, and then I saw the moon," said a kid who went by the name of Flash, presumably because he was the fastest runner in the school. Hector made as if to go after Joey, but Flash pushed him back.

"Hey," Flash said, "you don't have a Furman name yet. How 'bout we call you Cheeks?"

"Or how about Crack?" said another.

Hector kept his eyes on Joey. He wanted him to know that nothing had changed. "How about Coward?" Joey said by way of response to Hector's glare.

"All right," Antonini said, stepping in front of Hector and the group. "That's enough. Hector here already got a Furman name."

"What?" Flash asked.

"His name is Clinto Estemadera, 'cause he's a man of few words, like my man Clint Eastwood. Get it? Clinto Estemadera."

"Man, that name sucks," Flash said.

Antonini ignored him. "Fun time's over. Get out of here, all of you. Hit the showers."

"How about facing me in a grudge match instead of grabbing me from behind?" Hector shouted at Joey. His voice was shrill and not as menacing as he had hoped.

It took Joey a few seconds to realize Hector was talking to him. Joey looked at Antonini, befuddled. "What's a fudge match?"

"Grudge match," Antonini responded, trying not to laugh. "You and Clinto go at it with boxing gloves." Then to Hector, "We can set up a grudge match between you two, but not now, and not this week. Talk to me next week if you both are interested."

Joey said to Hector, "I'm not gonna waste my time in no boxing match with you. You got no bolas. Stay out of my face."

There were some *oohs* from the group, and then Antonini motioned for Joey to walk with him. "Why don't you take a breather before you head back?" he told Hector.

Hector sat on the edge of the track and began to pull out handfuls of grass. Maybe the anger in him would make its way through his arms and into the ground. He felt a pain on the side of his abdomen. He closed his eyes and then opened them when something cold touched his arm. Sansón was offering him a bottle of water.

Hector refused at first, but Sansón insisted. He opened the bottle and gulped down half of it. Hector knelt and waited to see if maybe he needed to vomit. It was a false alarm. He leaned back on his haunches. He picked up the bottle and drank the rest of the water.

"Small sips are better," Sansón said. Hector stared at him. Maybe Sansón would get the message and disappear. But Sansón was not moving. "You're out of shape."

"You think?"

"I do," Sansón responded, ignoring or not catching Hector's sarcasm. They looked in the direction of a backhoe moving across the back fields. "That's Yoda. He's going to the old fire station to dig up an old septic tank. He's looking for volunteers. I'm gonna do it. You should too."

"A septic tank." Hector sat back down and stretched his legs. Groups of kids were heading back to their dorms to shower and then move on to breakfast and the rest of the day. Hector saw Joey walking with three others, laughing.

"Yeah, man. Digging for two days will make your hands hard . . . for when you box Topo."

"Topo. That's his Furman name."

"Yeah. He looks like one of them moles." Sansón laughed. "Clinto's a good name. Antonini saved you from getting stuck with a bad name."

"When can we start training?"

Sansón's wide forehead wrinkled in deep thought. "I'll be honest with you. Technique will beat strength most of the time. But to get the kind of technique that could beat that kid's strength, you need to train for a couple of months, at least."

"I just outran him and I'm out of shape, like you say."

"You got clean lungs. But that don't matter when he hits you."

"Can you help me or not?"

"Yes. We have a deal, no? All I'm saying, next week is too

soon. Learning boxing takes a long time. And you'll need to get in shape, build lung power—"

"All I want is to hit him hard! A few good punches. It will make me feel better. I don't care if I lose the match. Can you teach me?"

Sansón looked at Hector for a long time. Hector could see in Sansón's face that he understood the need to hit. He had been there before. Sansón shook his head slightly with pity or disapproval. Hector didn't care. All he wanted was to have his hands explode on Joey's face.

"Yeah, man. I can teach you how to hit. That's easy. Come over by the gym after work detail. We be lifting weights with Mr. Díaz then. X-Man lifts with us. He'll set up the GM for you. He'll find a way to get Topo to fight you. Meantime, after breakfast, sign up for the same work details that I do. The work I do builds strength."

"Digging septic tanks?"

"Yeah. On Saturday, we'll do some technique stuff." Sansón scratched his bristly cheek. He looked embarrassed for what he was about to say. "Remember the deal we made?"

"Yeah." Hector sighed. "We can start tonight. Pick a book."

"You read with me," Sansón said, "and I show you how to punch."

"Enough for me to beat Topo?"

"No," Sansón said. "But enough for the vato to respect you."

Hector felt a knot tighten in his throat. He could care less about Topo's respect. What he wanted was for Topo to grovel. Today, he had tried and failed. Actually, he had ended up getting humiliated yet again, and now in front of the people he wanted to present himself as tough to.

So much for the new Hector.

CHAPTER 18

Hector made his way, painfully, to the large corrugated steel structure used as the Furman gym. That morning at breakfast he had added his name on the activities schedule wherever Sansón's name appeared. Weight lifting was at 4:00 p.m., and he was ten minutes late. The giant aluminum doors of the old airplane hangar were open, and he could see a volleyball game in progress. On one side of the gym were two thick ropes hanging from the rafters with kids crawling their way to the top. He walked on the side opposite the ropes. The heat inside was oppressive. The only ventilation came from the open doors and a few small window-like openings near the roof. The smell of sweat rose about nose high and stayed there. The shouts of the volleyball players bounced off the sides of the gym in loud echoes. All day long, as he sat through his assigned classes, he had looked forward to getting stronger. He imagined starting off slowly and increasing the weights each day. Whatever Sansón

recommended, he would double. He was looking forward to exercising his body. Maybe his body could give
him what his mind apparently couldn't: the fearlessness
he wanted and needed. All his head seemed to give him
was more things to worry about: life in a place like the U,
his mother and Aurora struggling on their own. Judge
Galvan was wrong—it wasn't that he had acted without
thinking. He had sat in the truck paralyzed with thinking
while his brother got killed.

"Clinto! Over here." A very pale, tall kid waved to Hector.
The first thing Hector noticed were eyebrows so blond they
were almost white. "I heard you were going to lift with us.
Come on, you're late!

"I'm X-Man." The kid extended his hand, and Hector took
it. He was surprisingly strong for someone who was all bone
and no muscle.

"You're the . . ."

"Yeah, I'm the guy that arranges the grudge matches.
Sansón told me about you."

"What do I have to do to set one up?"

"What's with you and this Topo kid?"

"Does it matter?"

"It might help me in convincing the kid to fight you. I was
there this morning. He didn't seem all that interested."

"He killed my brother."

"A grudge match ain't gonna help you with that, bro. Trust me, I know."

"Yes. It *will* help," Hector said firmly.

For a moment there, it looked as if X-Man was thinking about revealing something personal. Instead, he shook his head and began to put the dumbbells in order—from lightest to heaviest.

"He needs to know I'm not afraid of him," Hector almost shouted.

X-Man glanced up at Hector, a sly grin on his face. "*Who* needs to know *he's* not afraid?"

"Just tell me who can set this up if you won't do it."

"All right, all right. I'll do it. Do you have any money?"

"Sixty dollars."

"I'll need twenty."

"For what?"

"Can't have a grudge match without an RA present. Ten will go to Antonini and the other ten for me."

"What do you do?"

"I make the magic happen." X-Man stood and grabbed Hector's hands. He turned them and inspected the palms. "You don't know jack about fighting, do you?"

Hector yanked his hands away. "Just set the match. Next week."

"Let me give you some free advice. No offense, but unless

you got some hidden powers, you're no match for this Topo kid. Why don't you wait a month or more? You're not going anywhere, and neither is he. Build up some muscle, some lung power, put some calluses on your baby hands. Let Sansón teach you a few things."

"No. It has to be soon." After the grudge match, he had to kill Joey. Longer than that and he would self-destruct—eaten alive by his own anger.

X-Man continued. "And if you wait a while, you can make some money. Betting's not allowed, but it happens. You fight next week, no one is going to put any money on you. Fight next month when you bulk up a little, and maybe in between you do things to piss the kid off and then you'll build up some anticipation for the fight. Kids will bet, and you and me could make us a few bucks. Even if you lose, we win. Know what I mean?"

Hector liked the idea of pissing Joey off, getting under his skin and in his mind. And he knew for a fact that Joey was physically stronger than he was. Some kind of training would be good. But still, a month was too long. "Next week," Hector said.

"Okay. You the boss."

Hector looked at the iron weights and dumbbells stacked on the floor. The weights were all five and ten pounds and the heaviest dumbbell was twenty pounds. "That's it?"

"Yep. We also do a little jump roping."

"It's not exactly heavy lifting," Hector said, disappointed.

"The kind of lifting Mr. Díaz teaches is done with light weights."

"Mr. Díaz?" It took a moment to remember where he had heard that name. "As in the mind's flashlight?"

"Hey, how'd you know?

"An inmate at the U. He said he knew Mr. Díaz."

"Makes sense. The story about Mr. Díaz is that he spent a whole bunch of years in prison for killing someone, and then, when he came out, he got a job at Furman."

Hector said, "From one prison to another."

X-Man gave Hector a nasty look. "Think about how much a man can learn in an eight-by-twelve cell for twenty years and how much he can teach others. This lifting we're doing is something he learned in prison."

"Makes sense," Hector said.

X-Man ignored the sarcasm. "He lives on campus. In the apartments next to the administration office. Colonel Taylor and Old Lady Taylor live there and a few others. Mr. Díaz being one of them. He teaches history here. Hey, I was just thinking—I may have a way to get Topo interested in fighting you."

"Go ahead. Or do I have to pay for that too?"

"Ha! You're funny, Clinto. Listen, Topo's playing basketball with the Mayas tomorrow afternoon. I can get you in with the team they're playing against. When they put you in, get him pissed and challenge him again to put the gloves on with you. If he turns you down twice, people will start to think he's running from you. He'll have no choice but to fight you."

Hector thought about X-Man's words. "What makes you think he cares about what people think?"

"He likes it here," X-Man said. "He's found a home."

"Here? A home?"

"Don't look so surprised. Look at him."

Hector turned in the direction where X-Man pointed and saw Joey halfway up one of the ropes that hung from the rafters. He was being swung in circles by a kid twirling the rope from the ground. Joey was shouting and laughing, "¡Ay, cabrón! Párale, cabrón! I'm gonna puke on you, pendejo."

"He can like it here all he wants," Hector said. Then to himself he added, *He won't be here for long*.

"Shoot, I forgot the jump ropes. I'll be right back," X-Man said, taking off in a run.

Hector grimaced and rubbed his legs. No one said anything about rope jumping.

"You must be Hector," a man said behind him. "Glad you could join us. I'm Ismael Díaz." Except for the painful handshake, there was nothing about Mr. Díaz that indicated any kind of familiarity with violence—past, present, or future.

The guy looked like the kind of person who couldn't hurt a fly. Mr. Díaz said, "I talked to your teacher at Ysleta High earlier today. Mr. Lozano. He spoke highly of you. The teachers here wanted to get an idea of what you were studying back home so we can come up with an individual study plan for you. You've noticed, I'm sure, that you're more advanced than where we are. You'll still be going to the classes listed on your schedule, but we'll probably give you separate assignments that you can work on your own. We want to make sure you're not bored." Mr. Díaz stopped, waited for Hector's reaction. Hector forced a grin. Mr. Díaz continued, undeterred. "Mr. Lozano is going to send me the books you've been using."

"Okay," Hector said, not knowing what else to say. He couldn't very well tell the man not to bother. Keeping up with his studies was not high on his list of priorities.

"So, Alberto convinced you to give our weight-lifting program a try."

"Alberto?"

"Beto. Sansón. Sometimes I think it's just easier if the Furman staff uses the nicknames you guys give each other. You been baptized yet?"

"Clinto. Clinto Estemadera."

"Wonderful," Díaz said, laughing. "And you even got a last name."

X-Man came out of the back door of the gym with three jump ropes over his shoulder. Sansón lumbered behind him. X-Man threw one of the ropes to Hector. They were the kind that Aurora used to have when she was maybe eight years old: pink plastic handles and a rope of different colors.

"Ready, Clinto?" Sansón closed his fists and pretended to throw a punch at Hector.

Díaz walked to the side of the gym and began to unroll a poster or a map that had been tucked under his arm. He took masking tape out of his back pocket. Sansón and X-Man moved closer, and after a few moments, Hector did as well. The three of them stood in a horizontal line looking at what turned out to be a diagram of the human body's muscular system. "Alfred and Beto have seen this before," Mr. Díaz said to Hector, "but I thought it would be good to give you an overview of what we're trying to do here."

Hector stared at the sinewy red figure of a skinless man, his green eyes popping like peeled grapes. Then Mr. Díaz walked to the rack of dumbbells and grabbed the heaviest on the end. Effortlessly, Mr. Díaz demonstrated a series of lifts, and after each lift, he pointed to the muscles involved. "Your mind should be like a flashlight that shines directly on the major muscle group being used. When you lift, feel the tension there. When you rest, feel the relaxation there. When your mind drifts someplace else, bring it back to the muscles. Focus on the muscles you're using like a lion watches an intruder approach its den."

Hector stared at Sansón. *Where's the boxing?* he asked with hand and facial gestures. Sansón pointed back at Mr. Díaz.

"Any questions, Hector?"

How do I get out of here? Hector thought. He shook his head.

"Okay." Mr. Díaz clapped his hands. It was a signal that the lecture was over. X-Man and Sansón walked to the rack, and each grabbed a pair of dumbbells. X-Man's dumbbells were heavier than Sansón's, which made no sense. Then the two separated a few spaces from each other and began the weight-lifting routines. The whole thing reminded Hector of watching television with the sound off.

Hector stood, awkwardly, in the silence. He was supposed to pretend that his mind was a flashlight? How the hell was that going to help him beat the living daylights out of Joey? Well, at least there was silence. Since he got to Furman, there had been few places where he had found silence, and that included nighttime in his room with Sansón talking in his sleep. Hector picked up a five-pound dumbbell and began to lift it quickly from his thigh to his chest. This was easier than he'd imagined. Was this all he had to do? He looked at the serious expressions on X-Man and Sansón and tried not to laugh.

Mr. Díaz approached Hector. "Watch Sansón. See how he breathes?"

Hector focused on Sansón's flat nose. Sansón's nostrils flared with inhaled breath as the weight went up, closed slightly as he exhaled and the weight went down. It was all one movement, the breathing in and the lifting up, the breathing out and lifting down.

"Now you do it, Hector," said Mr. Díaz.

"This is supposed to make me stronger?" Hector couldn't help himself.

"Sansón told me you wanted to train for a grudge match," Mr. Díaz said.

Hector looked at Díaz, alarmed. Was he going to try to stop it?

"Don't worry. Officially, Furman is zero tolerance on violence. But we're not stupid. We need to let kids blow off steam. Boxing and other forms of competition will do that. The thing is, Sansón was right in telling you to come to this class. When you're in the ring, it's going to be chaos inside your head. It will be your ability to see and to stay calm that will help you survive and maybe even win. If you can see the opponent begin to throw a punch, you can avoid it, or you can counter with your own punch or both. And, believe it or not, these small weights will build up all the strength you need without making you sluggish. It doesn't take a lot of strength to knock someone out. Does that make sense?"

"I guess."

"This program is about *seeing*. Seeing clearly with their eyes and with their mind is what champions do. Okay?"

"Like in chess."

"Like in everything," Mr. Díaz said, smiling.

Five minutes later, Hector's arms hung lifeless and limp by his sides.

Mr. Díaz raised his hand. Sansón and X-Man stopped lifting. "Let's jump for ten minutes." X-Man put his dumbbells on the ground and began to dole out the jump ropes. Mr. Díaz demonstrated the technique. The rope zoomed over Mr. Díaz's head and under his feet in an invisible but perfect circle. The only thing that touched the ground were his tiptoes. He stopped and said to Hector, "This is different than the focus you had lifting. This is more about feeling a rhythm." Then, to everyone, "Let's do five sets of fifty with a thirty-second rest between sets."

Hector couldn't do more than five swings without the rope hitting his ankles. Then he remembered a rhyme in Spanish that Aurora used to sing when she jumped rope.

Tin Marín de don pingué, cucara macara, titere fué, yo no fuí, fue teté, pegale a ella que ella fué.

He repeated that over and over again, timing the speed of the rope's swing to the beat of the rhyme, and somehow made it to fifty without tripping once and without once thinking about Joey. It felt good, that little window of freedom. And it felt good to remember Aurora. He smiled and then pulled the smile back when he saw that Mr. Díaz was watching him.

But it was too late. Mr. Díaz was giving him a thumbs-up.

CHAPTER 19

The basketball court separated dorms A and B. Wooden bleachers stood on one side, and that's where everyone who wasn't playing sat to watch and, Hector noticed, to place bets on the teams. X-Man, who seemed to be everywhere, was at the bottom rung with a small notebook and the pen he usually kept behind his ear, playing the part of a bookie. Hector figured the money that kids used for wagers came from parents who could afford to send it.

The after-dinner basketball court was the only place at Furman that resembled the outside world. Teams were formed strictly in accordance with the color of the players' skin: Black, Brown, and White. The only kid who could play on either a Black team or a Brown team was a Native American boy who went by the Furman name of Lebanon (Hector had stopped trying to understand the logic behind Furman names). Although Lebanon's skin was more brown than black, he was also six foot one, and it occurred to Hector that maybe that had something to do with his ability to penetrate the racial divides.

Hector sat on the top rung of the bleachers watching a game between a Black team and a White team. Jerry, the RA, was the referee. Jerry walked around the court with a black whistle in his mouth. Hector heard him blow the whistle to start the game and to end the game. Other than that, Hector figured the only reason Jerry was there was to call 911 if a player went down and did not get up after ten minutes or so. Elbows, punches, kicks, tripping, and even biting were deemed part of the game. It didn't take long for Hector to understand that the after-dinner basketball games, or "street ball," as X-Man called it, was where kids *really* let off steam.

Hector saw Joey warming up with one of the Brown teams. It was hard for Hector to understand why Joey had taken to Furman like a fish to water. Maybe Furman was better than the slavery of addiction. Joey had been forced to detoxify. The poison of the drug had been sucked out of him, and now Joey seemed content—there was no other word to describe it. There he was joking around with the other players like he'd known them all his life. How Joey had managed to insert himself into the Mayas, a team that had probably been playing together for months, was beyond Hector's comprehension. Hector had to shell out five dollars just so X-Man could buy him ten minutes of play on the Carnales.

"Hey, Clinto." X-Man signaled to Hector. "You're on."

Hector and X-Man walked over to Tulito, the captain of the Carnales. Hector knew him from Mr. Díaz's American History class. Tulito looked at Hector while X-Man handed him a five-dollar bill.

"You a player?" Tulito asked Hector.

"Yeah," Hector responded with as much confidence as he could muster. It was more or less the truth. He had played basketball in grade school and in PE at Ysleta High. He had spent hours shooting baskets by himself after school. And there were those interminable games of H-O-R-S-E with Aurora.

"I'll sub you in the second half. Play forward so you don't have to dribble the ball. We need to get a lead first. Don't shoot. If you get the ball, pass it right away before anyone ties you up."

"I need to go in when that guy is playing." Hector pointed at Topo.

"The kid with the ball?"

"Yeah. Topo."

"No, man. You go in when we have a lead."

"No Topo, no five dollars." Hector glared at Tulito.

Tulito glared back and then broke into a smile. Five members of the Mayas were assembling at midcourt. Topo was one of them. "Looks like he's starting. Go ahead and start for me. Five minutes and then you're out."

X-Man pulled Hector to the side. "Don't do anything that gets you or Topo kicked out of Furman."

Hector nodded that he understood. The plan was to harass Joey. Let him know that Fili's death would not be forgotten. Let him recognize whose mind was superior. He walked to the middle of the court. Jerry, the referee, was ready to toss the ball in the air. Hector stood next to Joey, who was grinning, not one bit surprised to see Hector. "I'll take him," Hector said to the other Carnales, pointing at Joey.

"Too late to grow a pair, *Clinto*!" Joey snickered.

Hector was taller than all but three of the players on either team. The jump ball was tipped by the Carnales player. Hector jumped and recovered it. He held the ball for a few moments and waited for the rest of his team to spread out around the basket. Joey crouched defensively, his eyes locked on Hector's face, attempting to restrict Hector's movement. Hector faked a pass and dribbled away from Joey. He threw a long lob to an unguarded player under the basket who made an easy layup. The Carnales player pointed at Hector, thanking him for the pass.

Joey was bringing the ball back up the court with Hector guarding him, pawing at the ball. His teammates were shouting at Joey to pass, but he ignored them. Joey's dribble was slow and clumsy. When he tried to go around Hector, Joey lost control, and the ball rolled toward the sidelines. Hector and Joey both dove for it. Joey wrestled the ball away from Hector's hands, but not before the referee had blown his whistle. Jump ball.

Joey and Hector stood midcourt. The basketball game was a great idea. Hector was taller than Joey, and he was also, surprisingly, a better player. The objective had been harassment, but why not score on Joey as much as possible, to embarrass him? Jerry tossed the ball, and Hector easily tipped it to one of his teammates, who dribbled a few steps and shot a long three-point basket. Joey asked for the ball, but the Maya player bringing it in ignored him. Hector noticed that Joey was struggling to keep up. One of the Mayas shot from the three-point line. The ball hit the rim, and Hector rebounded. Hector shoved Joey out of the way with his shoulder and dribbled toward the basket. Joey went sprawling to the ground as Hector scored an easy two points. Joey was slow getting up, asking Jerry why there was no foul called.

Tulito called time-out from the sideline. Hector prepared himself to argue for more time. He was having fun at Joey's expense.

Tulito said, "You better get out before you lose it."

"Me?" Hector said. It was Joey who was getting rattled.

"Five more minutes. I can pay you later. We're winning, aren't we?"

"All right, but keep your cool."

What the hell was Tulito talking about? Couldn't he see that he was in control? He was revved up, yes, but fully in command of body and mind.

Joey demanded the ball, and one of the Mayas reluctantly passed it to him. Hector stood in front of him, waving his arms, keeping Joey from either passing or dribbling. There was saliva coming out of Joey's mouth. He had what looked to Hector like a panicked, deer-in-the-headlights look. Mayas were shouting at him to pass the ball. Hector moved in closer. Then, unexpectedly, Joey handed the ball to Hector. He leaned in and whispered in Hector's ear, "Your brother's head was nice and round like this ball. It felt so good to hit it with the bat. So good."

Then it happened. The heat that had been barely contained exploded. Hector took a step back and threw the ball at Joey. Joey managed to turn his face just enough to avoid getting hit in the nose. The ball bounced off Joey's cheek. Hector stood there, stunned, watching Joey spit out a tooth. Hector tried to say something, but his throat closed up on him and his eyes filled with water. Somewhere inside he felt the absence of his brother as if it were a gaping, dark, bottomless hole. His brother was gone, and now Hector understood that it would be forever. He quickly turned away from Joey and the other players staring at him so that they would not see the flood of snot and tears. He bit his tongue so as to keep all the noises of sorrow and anger inside of him. He walked off the court, slowly, trying to carry himself with some semblance of composure. He was halfway to his dorm when X-Man caught up to him.

"You all right?"

"Yeah. Why wouldn't I be?" Hector wiped his eyes and nose with his forearm.

"Man, Clinto! You were supposed to piss the kid off, not try to kill him."

"How long do I have before I get kicked out of Furman?" He had to figure out how to kill Joey before then. The hell with trying to own him.

"Yeah, ordinarily you'd be gone after that little stunt. You're in luck. I talked to Jerry, and he agreed not to tell the colonel. Jerry saw the kid whisper something to you. He knows you were provoked. But Jerry had to do *something* because of the rules."

"What?" Hector sat on the steps to his dorm. X-Man sat next to him. He forced himself to listen.

"First, Jerry's got to report the incident to someone on senior staff. I told him you were in our weight-lifting group with Mr. Díaz, and he agreed to tell him. That's good, man—all you'll get from Mr. Díaz is a lecture. I hope you listen to him before you self-destruct. But hey, it's your life. Second, you and Topo are working on the same outside detail tomorrow. You'll be digging the old septic tank."

Him and Joey out there alone with picks and shovels. Was that destiny or what?

"Sansón will be with you, so just go ahead and wipe that thought out of your mind. It's an old Furman strategy: put two kids that hate each other on the hardest, most aggravating job."

"Makes sense," Hector said. He wasn't trying to be funny, but X-Man laughed.

"I have some good news for you, if you're still interested. I got Topo to agree to a grudge match next week. I asked him in front of everyone, and as I suspected, he was afraid to look bad—especially after you busted his tooth."

"Didn't he look like a coward back there by not retaliating . . . after I busted his tooth?" Maybe something good had come out of that humiliating scene.

"No, man. He was in control. He came out looking strong."

And I came out looking weak, Hector said to himself.

"You still want to go through with the grudge match?" X-Man asked.

"What's the point?" He had just whacked Joey with a basketball, and Joey was still strong and he was still weak. And as for getting Joey to fear him? A boxing match wasn't going to do it.

X-Man looked intently at Hector. "That's right, dude. You got it. There *is* no point to it. You're not going to bring your brother back, no matter what you do to that kid."

"You know that flashlight Díaz talked about the other day?"

"Yeah."

"It's shining on Topo, and it's not moving."

"Well then, you're just plain certifiable. Why you doing this to yourself? Putting yourself in a damn straitjacket like that? There's a shrink who comes every Sunday. His name is Dr. Luna. You should go see him. I saw him for a few Sundays when *my* flashlight got stuck and I was within an inch of turning the damn thing off . . . permanently." X-Man went suddenly quiet. He looked as if he was remembering something painful. Then, "Dude, you gotta find a way to move on. When your flashlight's stuck like that, you're not *seeing*, like Mr. Díaz says, and seeing's the only way to free yourself."

X-Man sounded like a younger, paler version of Cortina. He tried to remember Cortina's exact words about getting out of his mental prison but couldn't. What he *could* remember was Joey's words back in the basketball court. What he *could* see was Joey killing his brother.

"What else is there to see?" Hector asked, forgetting that X-Man was there.

"You kiddin', right?" Hector did not respond, and X-Man continued, agitated. "You want to know what I see? I see a conveyor belt inside my head going around and around full of crap. I see the old lady who took me in as a foster kid and then I see myself stealing everything she had. I see the only girl who ever cared for me leaving me 'cause I chose dope over her. What crap do *you* see in your conveyor belt? Try shining your flashlight on *that* for a change!" X-Man took a deep breath, looked away in the direction of the basketball court. Hector noticed that his cheeks turned bright red just like Azi's when she got angry. After a few moments, X-Man stood and said, "You want the damn grudge match or not?"

"Yeah," Hector said. "Why not?"

X-Man turned around and stomped away. Hector closed his eyes, and imagined a conveyor belt. Joey was there. He was so big and heavy that the conveyor belt could barely move. But Fili was not far behind. In the distance, he could see Aurora holding a multicolored jump rope in her hand. The people in the conveyor belt elicited different emotions as they went around. He was familiar with the rage and the intense desire to destroy that came from Joey, but how strange that he had never before felt the moist sadness that Fili brought. Hector opened his eyes before Aurora could roll by. He couldn't stand to feel the guilt and shame she awakened.

He went inside the dorm. He knocked on Antonini's door,

and when no one answered, he opened it anyway. It took him only a few seconds to find what he was looking for. It was attached to a green ribbon and was hanging on a nail next to the door. It looked like the key Aurora used on her first roller skates. He walked to the inside entrance of the dorm and inserted the key into a black box next to the door. A light went from green to red. He noticed a similar box on the outside of the building. He tried the key there with the same result. Then he made his way over to dorm C and did the same. The key worked on all doors.

I've found a way to do what needs doing. When the time is right. I'm in control again.

CHAPTER 20

The following afternoon, Sansón, Joey, and Hector walked over to the old fire station. Hector and Joey each carried a shovel. Sansón carried a pick and a shovel in each hand and a one-gallon container filled with water in a small backpack. When they were getting the shovels and pick from the toolshed, Jerry said to Sansón, loud enough for Hector and Joey to hear, "Feel free to use violence if they try to kill each other."

Now they walked in silence, single file, with Joey in the lead, Hector in the middle, and Sansón lagging behind. Joey had shown up at the toolshed accompanied by Jerry, and his only communication to Hector was to snort and spit. With the shovel on his shoulder, Joey up ahead looked like one of Snow White's seven dwarfs on his way to work. Hector looked up and saw two buzzards flying in a clean blue sky. He saw Joey watching them, following the glide of the birds.

"They're waiting for you," Hector said to Joey.

Joey didn't turn around or respond. It would be so easy

to whack the back of Joey's head with a shovel. What was stopping him? The thought had crossed his mind once or twice that prison would be a life in hell. But there was also something cowardly about killing someone from behind. He stopped walking. Why had it never occurred to him that Joey had killed Fili like a coward?

A few minutes later, they reached the concrete foundation where the fire station had once stood. Joey and Hector peered down at a trench that went out for about twenty-five yards. Sansón caught up to them. He put the backpack with the water on the ground. Joey went to reach for it, but Sansón stopped him. "It's for later, when you really need it."

Joey stared at Sansón, questioning his authority. Sansón was just another Furman student, but Hector had observed that other students treated him with deference. It wasn't just his size and strength that earned him respect; it was the way Sansón carried himself. He walked and talked like Fili, without hurry or worry, as if he could handle whatever life threw at him. Hector knew that Joey would be the first to blink, and he did. Joey spat to the side and took off his gray regulation Furman T-shirt. He pointed to a backhoe a few yards away. "Why don't we use that?"

"Yoda used the backhoe to dig the trench as much as he could. The old cast-iron pipe is about a foot below there." Sansón peered into the trench. "We use shovels and picks to dig around the pipe. When we're done, Yoda will come and cut the pipe with a blowtorch and lift it out in pieces. I'm gonna dig over by the tank. You two work on the pipe. One here and the other one at the other end. When you meet each other in the middle, come over where I'm at."

Joey was the first to jump into the trench. Hector went to the other end.

"Hey, man," Joey yelled at Hector, "how come you never take off your shirt? You still got the mark I put on you?"

It was good to be out here with Joey. Whatever doubts or fears Hector had about killing Joey after the prison visit burned away in Joey's rotten presence. Hector jumped in the trench and started digging toward him. "Hey, Joey! How's Chavo doing? When he gets to be sixty, he should get one of those wheelchairs with a motor to zoom around."

"Even on a wheelchair, my brother's more man than you or your pinche dead brother ever was."

A minute later, Hector said: "Hey, do you still have the little cowboy outfit? You looked really cute in it."

This time Joey did not answer. Hector had struck gold. Was there something sacred about that picture? Hector stopped and looked up, half expecting to see Joey charging him with a shovel in the air. But all that Hector saw was Joey standing and grinning.

"What's the name of that hynita you have the hots for?

Cucaracha? Some weird name. I forgot. She was super bue-nota, man!"

Hector felt blood rise to his face. Now was the perfect time. Why wait? It hurt. It hurt to have that animal talk about Azi. The fact that he even thought about her was enough for Hector to wish him to die, die now, and die painfully. *I am in control*, Hector said to himself. He was about to shout another insult when he saw Joey begin to dig furiously.

"Whoever gets to the middle first has the biggest bolas!" Joey shouted. "Come on, puto, show me what you got!"

"That's stupid. That's what a little kid with a pea brain would say."

Hector watched Topo for a few seconds, and then he took off his T-shirt, tossed it to the side, and began to dig with all his might. He dug until his shovel struck iron and then dug on the side of the pipe as he could see Joey doing. Now and then they would both lift their heads at the same time and put their heads down and dig faster. There was sweat stream-ing down Hector's forehead into his eyes. *This is ridiculous*, Hector thought. *It's like we're back in grade school.*

"Hey, Hector!" Joey was yelling. "Where's the middle? How we gonna know who has more bolas if we don't know who gets there first?"

"The middle is by that brick right there!"

"No way. That brick is closer to your side."

Hector jumped out of the trench. He walked back to his end and proceeded to walk to the foundation, where the trench started. He counted every step out loud. Joey sat on the edge of the trench and watched Hector intently like someone who expected cheating.

"It's eighty-four steps long," Hector announced when he reached Joey's end. "Half of eighty-four is forty-two. I know you're not smart enough to figure that out, so you have to trust me on that."

"I got all the smart I need right here," Joey said, grabbing his crotch.

Hector counted forty-two steps and marked the spot with the brick.

Sansón leaned on his shovel and shook his head. But Hector could tell that he was enjoying himself.

"I told you that brick was closer to your side," Joey commented.

They both jumped in the trench and grabbed their shovels.

Sansón shouted: "¿Listos? Uno, dos y . . . tres!"

It occurred to Hector as he saw Joey advance toward the brick with a speed and energy that he could not compete against, that the Furman kids had aptly named Topo. The kid was a topo, a furry, round, squinty-eyed, and pointy-eared mole who spent his life in a hole excavating dirt. Hard as he tried, Hector was not going to dig faster or better than Topo.

He was ten feet from the middle when Joey jumped out and stretched on the ground next to the brick. Hector finished and lay opposite Joey on the other side of the trench.

"I have the huevos," Joey said, out of breath. "You can have your pinche brains. I have the huevos."

Hector tried to come up with a response, but his pinche brains were as exhausted as everything else in his mortal being.

Sansón came by and handed the container of water to Joey, who sat up and drank until Sansón stopped him. When Hector had finished drinking, Sansón inspected the trench. He came and sat next to Hector. "We might finish the whole detail today. It was supposed to be a two-day job."

"Let's just relax, man. Suavecito, ¿qué no? We can finish tomorrow." Joey was lying down. Hector could tell that he was watching the two buzzards.

"That septic tank should be at the end of the pipe. I can't find it," Sansón said. "You guys take a break. I'm gonna finish."

Joey stood and grabbed his shovel. He looked at Hector sprawled on the ground. "Get up, pendejo. If we all dig, we can get back early."

Topo, dumb as he was, had a point. The sooner you finished your work detail, the sooner you could enter unscheduled time. Hector envisioned taking a shower in rare privacy and then maybe a short nap before dinner. He had not slept more than two hours the night before. "You want a little extra time to practice your basketball skills?" Hector said to Joey as he slowly got up. Joey ignored Hector's remark. *You need to have some intelligence to recognize sarcasm,* Hector said to himself.

Sansón had dug out a circular area about four feet deep and three yards in diameter. The three of them stood inside the circle. "There's a concrete tank underneath here." Sansón tapped his foot on the ground.

"Full of mierda," Joey added.

"We just gotta clear the dirt on top and around it so Yoda can lift it out with the backhoe. I'll loosen the dirt with the pick and you two can shovel. But go easy. Yoda said the tank's old and could give way."

"Let me use the pico," Joey said.

Sansón looked at Joey, considering. "Despacito," he said, handing him the pick.

Hector and Sansón watched Joey gently loosen the dirt with the pick before they started shoveling. Soon, they were all working quietly, efficiently, like a professional crew. Hector's mind went to his father's garden behind their house. His father and Fili would work together pulling out weeds and plucking the chilis when they were ready. They too worked in silence, absorbed in their own thoughts.

There was the sound of steel hitting rock. Joey said, "Pinche piedra."

Sansón and Hector looked up to see Joey lift the pick over his head. "No!" Hector and Sansón shouted at the same time. But the warning was too late. Joey brought the pick down on a round piece of concrete sticking out from the ground. There was a ripping, cracking, explosive sound, and then the earth opened up and Hector was swallowed up by darkness. He felt himself drop into a substance the texture of oatmeal. When his feet finally touched ground, he pushed himself up and saw that he was immersed up to his eyes in a foul-smelling, dark mush. He stood on tiptoes and was barely able to clear his mouth and nose to breathe. He saw Sansón holding the edge of the tank with his fingertips, his mouth just above the semi-liquid waste.

Hector looked around. Joey was gone. Then in a far corner he saw two hands sticking out desperately, trying to grab something, anything. Unlike Hector, Joey was not tall enough to get his mouth out of the muck even if he stood on tiptoes. Hector turned quickly and made sure that Sansón was not looking. He wasn't. No one would ever know if he made his way to the struggling Joey and pushed his head down. He watched Joey's fingers twitch for a few moments. Joey was drowning. Hector didn't have to do anything. He could simply watch the kid swallow mierda and die. Things would be balanced. Maybe the spirit of his father had cracked the septic tank the way Joey had cracked Fili's head. Except . . . damn, why did he have to think of his father just then? Papá would not let Joey drown. He wouldn't stand by like a coward. He'd kill Joey face-to-face, yes, in a fair fight. What did his father say in the dream: *You got things to do, do them.* Hector never imagined that saving Joey would be one of those things, but unfortunately, his father was telling him that it was.

Hector reached out and grabbed one of Joey's hands.

He could feel the panic in Joey's grip. Joey was pulling and dragging, making it impossible for Hector to lift him. He moved in back of the jerking Joey and lifted him by the armpits. Joey began to cough and gasp as soon as his mouth was out of the water. On tiptoes, slowly, Hector took Joey to the edge of the tank next to Sansón. Joey grabbed the edge and began to cough.

Sansón tried to pull out of the hole, but even his strength was not enough. It was impossible.

"I can climb on your shoulders and get out. Then I pull you out," Hector suggested.

"You won't be able to pull me. I'm too heavy."

Hector waited for Joey to finish vomiting and then said, "Listen carefully or we'll all die here. I'm going to lift you up enough so you can put your knees on Sansón's shoulders.

Then slowly, one leg at a time, you stand on Sansón and pull yourself out. You understand?"

Joey nodded.

Sansón crouched, submerging his head in the pestilent soup for a moment while Hector lifted Joey onto Sansón. When Joey was out, Sansón went under again, and Hector climbed on his shoulders. Hector pulled himself out. Joey was on the ground, sticking his finger down his throat and gagging.

"How do we get you out?" Hector asked Sansón.

"The shovel," Sansón said, trying to clear his mouth with the back of his hand.

He lowered a shovel to Sansón, but the hole was so deep that he could not get enough leverage to pull Sansón out.

"Hold me so I don't fall in," Hector said to Joey. Joey stood and grabbed Hector's waist. Hector had never touched an eel before, but he imagined they felt like Joey's arms on his torso. Sansón held on to the end of the shovel and tried to use his feet to climb out, but that nearly toppled Hector and Joey back into the hole. The shovel was not going to get Sansón out.

"Go get Yoda," Sansón said. The smell was so overpowering that Hector felt like he would pass out at any moment.

"How about that thing on the backhoe? That could work," Joey said.

Hector turned in the direction of Joey's gaze and saw a thick chain dangling from the bucket of the backhoe. "Let's try it." Joey unwrapped the chain and dragged it back to the pit. They lowered an end slowly to Sansón.

"Sit down and dig your feet into the dirt. Both of you hold on to it."

Joey wrapped the chain around his waist, and Hector behind him did the same. They buried their feet deep in the dirt, and then Sansón began to pull. For a moment there, it looked as if Sansón's weight would drag Joey and Hector into the tank, but Joey held on, every muscle in his body looking as if it were about to burst. Hector in turn held on to Joey as if his own life depended on it. When Sansón's upper body was safely on the edge of the pit, the two of them fell back, all strength drained from them.

Sansón threw one leg over the edge and then dragged the other one slowly out. The three of them lay on the ground faceup. Hector saw the same two buzzards circling above. The sky was a darker shade of blue now.

"Not today, pinches pájaros!" Joey muttered. Sansón laughed first and then Hector.

On the way back, Joey waited for Sansón to pull away out of earshot. He said to Hector, "You saved my ass." It was more like a question than a thank-you.

"I'm going to kill you with my own hands," Hector said. "I'm going to bash your brains in."

"Bring it," Joey responded without anger.

They caught up to Sansón, and the three walked back together.

CHAPTER 21

Hector sat by the side of Sansón's bed reading *The Old Man and the Sea*. It was raining outside, and Hector had brought the book to the infirmary. The day after they fell into the septic tank, Sansón had been diagnosed with dysentery. It was Sunday now, three days later, and the fever had finally subsided. Hector's voice was the steady monotone of someone who was not thinking about the meaning of the words:

I wish I could feed the fish, he thought. He is my brother. But I must kill him and keep strong doing it.

"Too bad the boy's not with him," Sansón interrupted.

Hector asked, "Why?"

"The boy could help him, ¿verdá?"

"I think the old man is supposed to struggle with the fish alone."

"He could fight the fish alone, but least he'd have the boy to talk to. So he don't be talking to himself like a loco."

"Talking to the boy wouldn't have helped him," Hector asserted.

"No, ese, talking to the boy woulda given him strength. The old man wished the boy was there. He even said so in the book, ¿qué no?"

Sansón paused as if he had just come upon something important. Hector saw Sansón's otherwise-opaque eyes glimmer for an instant and then heard him say, "Maybe the old man's not talking to himself. Maybe he's talking to the boy, pretending in his head the boy was there. Could be the boy's what kept him pulling the tuna. Maybe he never gave up on the tuna 'cause of the boy."

Sansón extended his arm, and Hector handed him the book. Sansón began to turn the pages, looking for the passage that would prove his point. Hector looked at the other two empty beds in the infirmary. By all accounts, Joey should be in one of those beds. It was Joey who'd swallowed the infected water. And yet, Joey was out there as if nothing had happened. Hector had seen him playing with a German shepherd puppy on his way to the infirmary. What happened out there? Why hadn't he let Joey drown? Hector hadn't quite figured it out. Yes, it would have been cowardly to watch Joey die like that, but it was more than that. Did he want Joey to feel indebted to him? If Joey was grateful, he didn't show it.

The one thing Hector knew for certain was that saving Joey's life only increased his desire to wring his neck. Go figure. X-Man was right. He was certifiable ... or quickly getting there.

"Mira," said Sansón, "here's the part where he wishes the boy was with him." Sansón began to read: *"I ... wish I had the boy. To ... help me and ... to ... see this."*

Hector didn't answer. Inwardly, however, he smiled. Sansón was right. The old man needed the boy.

Sansón closed the book and placed it on the nightstand.

"You done with the reading lesson?" Hector asked.

"Thanks, man. We never did the boxing training. You still want to fight Topo?"

"Yeah," Hector said. "It's on for Thursday."

Sansón was quiet for a few moments. When he spoke again, he was looking at the ceiling. "You and Topo are like the old man and the tuna. You're like hooked together."

Hector smiled. There was a little light inside Sansón's head, and once in a while it shone. "Yeah, could be. In a way," Hector admitted. Then Hector wondered: Was he like the old man being dragged to his death, or was he more like the hooked fish? If he was like the old man, he could just let go of the line that tied him to Joey. If he was the fish, his only chance would be to pull Joey into the deep waters of death.

Sansón grinned. Then his face turned serious. "What happens at the end, Clinto?"

"What do you mean?"

"At the end of the book. Who wins, the old man or the tuna?"

"You know. We read the book in class."

"Tell me again."

"The old man wins," Hector said. "He makes it to shore. He pulls the fish all the way in after all those days out there."

"The tuna's just bones."

"I think the guy who wrote the book would say that's a victory."

"No, man, that guy be wrong. They both lose."

Sansón closed his eyes. Just when Hector thought he had fallen asleep, he opened them and said, "I like it when the old man didn't want to disappoint the boy. Just like me, ese. My carnalitos back home, my mami, my old man in prison— not wanting to disappoint them gives me strength." Sansón's eyes suddenly filled with tears. He wiped them with his hand. "How about you, Clinto?"

"What?"

"You have anyone you don't want to disappoint?"

That was the question Hector tried to shoo away whenever it came up. How much more disappointment could he pile on his mother, on Aurora, and even on Azi? What would happen to them when he was in prison, or dead? When he was unable to dismiss those questions, he told himself that revenge was a duty he owed to Fili. Or maybe . . . it occurred to Hector just then, looking at Sansón's glistening eyes, his hatred for Joey was stronger than his love for his mother and sister.

Hector stood abruptly.

"I'll come by tomorrow," he said. Sansón raised his hand to stop him, but Hector turned around quickly and went out the door.

Hector ran out of the infirmary and then stopped. He turned and saw a small wooden structure a few yards away from him. It looked almost like a large toolshed, except one of the windows had an air conditioner that was running. Hector walked around the structure. On the door, which was hidden from public view, Hector read:

Dr. Oscar Luna

Sundays 12:00 p.m.—4:00 p.m.

Fill out card and slip under door for appointment,

Dr. Luna will contact you confidentially

Or knock if sign is on open.

There was a plastic bag with index cards and a pencil stuck to the door with a thumbtack. A laminated sign had been flipped to read *Open*. It was hard to believe that anyone at Furman would voluntarily talk to a psychologist, but X-Man had admitted doing it when his flashlight was stuck. Should he talk to Dr. Luna? Wasn't there something certifiably wrong with him? He felt as if his mind was coming unglued, unhinged. How could he prefer going to prison over his family? His flashlight was stuck in the worst way and it hurt, but he needed it to be stuck. For a moment, Hector thought of filling out a card. How would Dr. Luna get back to him confidentially? There were no phones in the dorms. Dr. Luna would have to use an RA or Lucy in Colonel Taylor's office. Hector stepped away from the door and went to the window closest to the door. The window's curtains were partially open, and Hector could see a man sitting typing on a desktop computer. Hector moved away quickly and then looked in again carefully. The man, it had to be Dr. Luna, was heavy, mostly bald, and older than any other staff member at Furman. He looked a little like Frank, his boss at the Piggly Wiggly. Hector watched Dr. Luna open the top drawer of a metal file cabinet opposite the desk and place a green folder in there. Hector saw Dr. Luna lock the file cabinet and put the key under a small sculpture of a flying eagle. He moved away from the window before Dr. Luna turned around.

Hector ran to the gym. Lifting the dumbbells and jumping rope seemed to be the only things that could quiet his mind. Sansón's words had stirred memories of home, and these filled him with a mixture of loneliness and yearning. Memories that he had struggled to forget began to move inside and seek the light of day. They were like the tender tendrils from the bean seeds that Aurora planted in paper cups. He stopped to watch a basketball game going on. Then something made him turn toward dorm C. There was Joey coming out alone and walking quickly, as if he was late for an important meeting. Hector watched him for a moment and then followed him. Joey was headed toward the infirmary. Had dysentery suddenly hit him? Was that why he was hurrying? There's no way he was visiting Sansón. But Joey walked past the entrance to the infirmary.

"I'll be damned!" Hector exclaimed. *Joey is seeing Dr. Luna.*

"Talking to yourself, Clinto?" Jerry quipped as he walked by.

"Hey, can I ask you a question?" Hector said, catching up to Jerry. "Do . . . I mean . . . are students ever, you know, *required*, to see . . . Dr. Luna?"

Jerry's knowing smile told Hector he knew why he was asking. Maybe he had also seen Joey walk in the direction of Dr. Luna's office. "Some of the students are addicts—alcohol, drugs, you name it. The physical cravings may be gone, but the mental ones are still there. They are *required*, as you put it, to see Dr. Luna so he can help them with the mental side of addiction."

"Makes sense," Hector said. The phrase had become one of his favorite expressions at Furman.

"If you want to be *required* to see him, that could be arranged."

"No. That's all right." Hector was about to say that he was no addict, although revenge felt a lot like a physical craving. "I was just curious."

"By the way, I know you haven't talked to Díaz about the basketball incident. You need to do it. Like today. He's over by the gym. I just saw him."

"All right."

Hector started again in the direction of the gym, but when Jerry was out of sight, he turned around and walked in the opposite direction. He couldn't talk to Mr. Díaz, not today. His thoughts were jumbled, scattered. He was agitated. He wondered what Joey was telling Dr. Luna. People talked to psychologists about their inner secrets, the ones they didn't even know they had until they popped up during the sessions. What were Joey's secrets? What was Joey afraid of? Dr. Luna must have known. The way to own Joey was to know his secrets and his fears and then hold this knowledge over him.

Without realizing, Hector found himself at the entrance to the library. He went in. The twenty computer terminals in the library were all occupied. It took Hector a moment to remember that students were allowed one hour of internet on Sundays. He was about to head back outside again when he heard his Furman name called out.

"Clinto, come here!" It was X-Man at the far end of the library. Hector made his way there. "You can have this one. I'm almost done. Just gotta kill this guy."

Hector did not tell X-Man that he had no intention of using the internet. But he had no place to go. He pulled up a chair and sat next to X-Man. On the screen, a woman dressed in a leopard bikini was shooting lasers out of her hands at a three-headed monster. *Must be another way to let off steam.* A stream of green goo came out of one of the three heads, and the leopard woman began to slowly melt.

"Oh, crap!" X-Man shouted. "I just got zapped."

"That was you? The woman?"

X-Man shrugged. "You have your fantasies. I have mine."

"Okay."

X-Man pushed his chair back and offered the terminal to Hector. "Knock yourself out, Clinto. Oh, I meant to tell you. There's people willing to put money on you. Not many, but enough to make your fight with Topo interesting."

"Yeah?"

"Yeah. Rumor's been spreading that you threw Topo into a cesspool."

"It was a septic tank, not a cesspool, and I didn't throw him in."

"Shhh! Betting is all about the buzz. Let the buzz happen, man."

X-Man jogged out of the library. Hector stared at the blue screen. He knew that there were sure to be emails waiting for him. How strange that he would rather fight Joey than read an email from Aurora. He feared the hurt that he would feel from her words more than the pummeling he was bound to get from Joey next Thursday. But Sansón's question was lodged in his chest like an obstruction that would not let him breathe: *You have anyone you don't want to disappoint?*

Hector took a deep breath, got himself ready for the pain that was about to come, and signed on to his email account. As expected, there were two emails from Aurora. The first one was written the day after he left for Furman and the second one the day before. There was also one email from Azi. Hector opened the first email from Aurora.

Hey bumhead,

Why you try to leave without saying goodbye? Don't worry, Mami and I understand. Please write to us whenever they let you write. Mami needs to hear from you.

Write soon. Miss you.

Aurora

Then he read the second one:

Hector—why haven't you written? Mami was so worried that she had me call to see if you were okay. I talked to some grumpy lady who said you arrived safely and were still alive as far as she knew. She said phone calls were not allowed the first month and internet only once a week for an hour. Just write us a couple of lines during that hour. How hard can it be? Don't make it harder on Mami than it already is. The news here is that Manny figured out a way for us to move to Socorro as soon as school is over. Manny gave us two thousand dollars from what was left over from Fili's insurance after he paid for the burial. He's fixing Fili's truck and already got a buyer for thirteen thousand. That's rent for a year, Manny says. Problem is, I can't get Mami interested in Socorro. She says here she can walk to work, that Socorro was Fili's dream, et cetera. If you tell her that you want to live there when you get out— she'll be interested again. Tell her Socorro is where you want to pursue happiness like you said in your speech. I'm doing okay in school except for algebra. Azi's doing her best to help me, but it could be I'm a helpless case.

Write soon,

Aurora

Happiness. It seemed like an eternity since he'd last heard that word or thought about it. *Happiness is the fulfillment of duty*, he remembered from his speech. The only problem was figuring out which duty to fulfill. Aurora's email tugged at him and called him home just like he knew it would. But was that tug and call stronger than the duty to humiliate and kill Joey? Hector hit reply and began to type:

Hey Aurora,

Sorry I haven't written. Furman does restrict outside access. I don't know why. Maybe so we can see quicker that this is where we're going to be for a while. I'm doing okay. Mr. Lozano has been in touch with the teachers here, and I'm doing a lot of independent studies. The place keeps me busy with classes and working. We get up at six and run three miles. I'm also doing some weight lifting in the afternoons. Almost every hour of the day is scheduled for us here. Don't worry about me. I'm making the best of it. You need to convince Mami that Socorro is good for you. You won't be living in the projects while you go to high school. It's not safe. I'm proof that it's not safe for you. I promise you I will write to her and say that to her as soon as my head clears a little more. She'll understand.

Take care, carnalita,

Hector

Hector sat there staring at the screen and then hit send. *As soon as my head clears a little more.* That was a lie. His head didn't seem like it would ever be clear again. He sat staring at Azi's email address. Did he have the strength to read her words? Thinking about Azi made him lonely. He knew that from the many sleepless nights at Furman. He felt he was already walking on fragile ground that would crack open at any moment. Azi's words could be the extra weight that sank him. He thought about printing her email and reading it on a day that was lighter, less emotional. Or maybe he was being a coward yet again?

Again? When had he stopped being a coward? Instead of opening Azi's email, Hector navigated to the Maestro I site and logged in. Immediately, he was filled with nostalgia. How many hours had he spent beating and getting beaten by the program until he reached the highest level? He checked his history of matches and saw his ascendancy over the past two years from a level 4 player to a level 8. The highest he could go on Maestro I was level 10, and if he got there, Hector would be playing world tournament matches against the world's grandmasters. Hector looked at the round white clock on the wall. He had a good half hour of time before he had to cede the terminal to someone else. Hector was tempted. A quick match just for old times' sake. On the other hand, chess was a slippery slope to the brainy, cowardly Hector he was trying to leave behind. Hector's deliberations were interrupted by a notification that he had a message. Hector clicked on the messages function of Maestro I. It was Elbereth. Hector hesitated a moment and then double-clicked on her name.

ELBERETH:

Greetings, Chaturanga! I haven't seen you on Maestro for eons. Where have you been?

Hector froze. How should he respond? Another lie? Why? Elbereth was a phantom he would never meet. He could be whoever he wanted to be with her, say whatever he wanted to say, including the truth.

CHATURANGA:

I no longer play chess.

ELBERETH:

What? Are you serious? I hope you're kidding.

CHATURANGA:

I'm not kidding. Things happened. I deleted
chess from my life.

ELBERETH:

Deleted?

CHATURANGA:

It's the only word I could think of. Cut off?
Removed?

ELBERETH:

You made a decision not to play anymore?

CHATURANGA:

Yes.

ELBERETH:

But it's not as if you don't love chess anymore?

Hector reflected. In all his days of playing chess, he had never referred to his excitement and dedication to the game as love. But it was love, wasn't it? A form of love. Chess was like a friend who challenged him and made him feel special and kept him company when he felt alone.

CHATURANGA:

It's not good for me to play chess right now.

ELBERETH:

The one thing I know for sure, Chaturanga, is that you and chess belong together. You can't just **delete** something you love out of you. You can try, I guess, but all you'll be doing is hurting yourself. I have the feeling that we're not just talking about chess here, are we? What else are you trying to delete? You're not talking about deleting yourself, as in suicide? Or killing another person . . .

Hector moved the computer's pointer over the red button that would end the conversation and clicked on it. How did messaging with this stranger become so intimate and full of emotion all of a sudden? He had not read Azi's email because he was afraid of what he might feel and ended up worse with Elbereth. Another mistake. The whole thing had backfired.

You can't just delete something you love out of you. What else are you trying to delete? Suicide? Killing another person? Who the hell was Elbereth to ask him those questions? The last thing he needed was for a fantasy to turn real. He felt raw and vulnerable, as if someone had busted a concrete covering in his chest and now everyone could see all the stinking stuff he was lugging around.

Hector logged off from Maestro I and then went back to his email account and printed Azi's email without reading it. He folded it and tucked it in his back pocket. He went outside and set off on a run. He had an hour or so before dinner, and he needed to be alone. He went around a group of students kicking a soccer ball. He saw Mr. Díaz and X-Man in the back of the gym. Díaz waved at him, but Hector kept running.

He was in no mood to hear a lecture about the damn flashlight.

The flashlight was going on and off, its light dimming, the battery's power about to expire. He had to find a way to recharge. Joey. Seeing him would do it.

CHAPTER 22

The following days, Hector had more energy than he knew what to do with. It was a restless, wasteful energy that seemed to pull him in different directions all at once. One moment he was ready to read Azi's email, and the next he was shadowboxing in his room, punching an imaginary Joey. On Wednesday afternoon, Mrs. Alvarez kicked him out of English class when she thought he was laughing at a student mumbling through *Hamlet*. He wasn't laughing *at* the student. He was recognizing the truth in Shakespeare's words: *Thus conscience makes cowards of us all*. He laughed because that was exactly what he needed to hear: To stop being a coward, he had to get rid of his conscience. Conscience included the things and people in his past that he loved. Elbereth was wrong. You *could* delete something or someone you loved.

Hector did not bother to explain to Mrs. Alvarez why he'd

laughed. He was happy to go outside. Sitting in a desk inside a classroom with thirty-three kids was asphyxiating. He headed to the gym to lift weights and jump rope and hit the sandbag that X-Man had dug out of the equipment room. He did not expect to see Mr. Díaz waiting for him there.

Hector waited for Mr. Díaz to jump right into the famous lecture, but instead Mr. Díaz said, "Thought you might want some boxing pointers."

"What?"

"I just came from the infirmary. Looks like Sansón will be getting out later today. He feels bad that he hasn't been able to keep his end of the bargain. You've been reading to him, but he hasn't trained you—for your grudge match tomorrow."

"You know."

Mr. Díaz pointed to the bottom bleacher. When he and Hector were sitting down, he continued. "I'll let you in on a little secret. Here at Furman we try to let the students make their own choices without too much interference from us teachers and staff. But that doesn't mean we don't know what's going on. We even try to influence those choices in hidden, manipulative ways, like assigning students to work on certain work details or pairing them with certain roommates. Things like that."

Hector was silent. Sansón, he understood, was supposed

to be a good, calming influence on him—but it hadn't quite worked out that way. "You know boxing?" Hector asked, changing the subject.

"A little." Mr. Díaz remained seated. Hector guessed the lecture was about to start.

Hector stammered, "Jerry asked me to talk to you . . . about hitting Joey . . . José Mendez . . . on the face with a basketball . . . on purpose. I got angry."

"Cortina, the inmate you saw, we were cellmates for a few years. We've sent him a lot of kids over the years. He says you're the only kid who's ever asked him the one question that needs asking."

"What question?"

"How do I live with courage?"

"I didn't ask him that."

"Yes, you did. He didn't say how he answered. Can you tell me? I'm curious."

Hector tried to remember Cortina's words. What exactly did he say? "The first step is to give up on revenge."

Mr. Díaz laughed. "Sounds like Cortina. Very practical."

"You don't agree."

"I think everyone needs to come up with their own answer to that question. But I think that, even before that, it's good to know about courage. There are different kinds. Some are more important than others. You, for example, already have a certain kind of courage. Sansón said you saved José Mendez's life at the septic tank."

"I didn't save . . ." How did Sansón know? He couldn't have seen anything with his face against the edge of the ditch.

"He saw you bring José to the edge where he could hold on to something. He could see that José was too short, someone would have had to lift him so he could breathe. You acted with courage. It also took courage to tell Judge Galvan the truth. And God only knows it takes courage to listen to Sansón read."

Mr. Díaz and Hector laughed at the same time.

Then Mr. Díaz got serious again. "But there's another courage, the most important kind, that I hope you find here at Furman."

Hector waited for Díaz to tell him, but after a long moment of silence, it was clear that Mr. Díaz's lecture or moral lesson was over. Mr. Díaz stood and then Hector did as well. Mr. Díaz walked over to Hector and showed Hector where to place his hands when boxing. "Imagine there's a spring here inside your right hand. Use that spring to jab when Joey comes swinging at you. And move around, like when we jump rope, on your toes, not flat-footed. The right jab to the face and moving is what you'll need to do to survive."

"I'd like to do more than just survive."

"It takes a combination of intelligence and courage to win a boxing match. You have both, but you haven't had the opportunity to put them together. It takes practice. I know how José will fight you. I've seen lots of kids like him fight. He's going to come after you like a tornado. He's a street fighter, and he's going to swing with wild, killer punches. Street fighting is fighting crazy and fast with all you got so the other guy can't even respond. He's going to be looping punches from the side, so what you need to do is watch his arms as they begin to move and then jab. The middle path to his face will be wide open. Ignore the glove coming at you, and place your eyes on his eyes. Keep moving and punching the front of his face. Eventually, his arms will tire, and maybe then you can get one or two good hits."

"Why are you telling me all this?"

"For a long time, we went back and forth about whether we should allow students to hit each other. We finally decided to allow grudge matches—"

"So kids can let off steam. I know, you told me."

"And because sometimes they teach the students something important about violence and revenge and about the highest form of courage."

"What?"

250

Mr. Díaz touched Hector's shoulder. "That's for you to figure out. Good luck, Hector."

At around three on Thursday morning, a sleepless Hector was going over his conversation with Mr. Díaz. Mr. Díaz had said that he, Hector, had courage. Imagine that! Someone had seen a courage in him that he hadn't seen before. Then Mr. Díaz had said that he believed that Hector had intelligence and courage . . . and that triggered a memory about his father and Fili.

Papá was home in bed, an oxygen tank next to him. Fili sat beside him reading an article about wild mustangs from an old *National Geographic*. Hector was walking to his room when he heard Fili trying to pronounce the word *equine*. Hector stood outside his parents' bedroom listening.

"Eee-queen?" Fili said. "What does it mean?"

"*Equeen?*" Papá imitated. Fili and Papá laughed. "Don't sound right."

Hector said from outside the hall, "It's *e-quine*. Pronounced like *line*. It means pertaining to a horse."

"There you go," Papá said. "Hector, get in here and teach your brother how to read." Hector stepped into the bedroom.

"Equeen," Fili said to himself, and laughed again.

His father pointed to the end of the bed. "Sit, Hector. I want to tell you a story." Hector did as his father asked and waited. Then his father said slowly, as if savoring every word, "Those mustangs we're reading about remind me of this yeguita I used to ride when I about your age, Hector. She didn't have much meat on her, but man, could she fly."

"Yeah?" Fili's voice was hoarse. He had been reading, or trying to read, to Papá for more than an hour.

"Cometa was her name. She belonged to the owner of the ranch. But I raised her from birth and trained her."

"How fast was she?" Hector smiled. Fili knew how to make Papá happy.

"Ooof," Papá replied. "She was so fast that if you yelled to someone a block away, she'd be there before he heard you."

Even Hector couldn't keep himself from laughing.

"Hector, I want to ask you something."

Hector looked first at Fili and then at his father. His father grabbed the oxygen mask beside him and inhaled and exhaled three times. When he took the mask off, Papá said to Fili, "I could use some of that tonic."

Fili reached for the bottle of tequila under the bed and poured two fingers into a glass. "Don't tell your mother," Papá said to Hector after downing the contents of the glass in one gulp.

Hector shook his head, pretending to disapprove. Everyone

in the house knew Papá medicated himself with tequila every twenty minutes or so. "What I want to ask you is about something I heard." His father coughed and gasped for breath. Fili offered him the oxygen mask, but Papá waved it away. After a few moments, he continued. "Manny, down at the shop, told me once that when the Indians in Mexico first saw the Spanish soldiers in their horses, you know, when they first came to Mexico, that the Indians were afraid because they thought the horses and the soldier were one: one beast—half horse, half man."

"I saw one of those in a movie once. Remember, Hector, when we took Aurora for her birthday? The bottom part was a horse and the top was a man."

"Centaurs," Hector said. "They're from mythology."

"Meet-o-logy," Fili stammered. "What's that?"

"They're not real. People made them up to explain things that . . . are difficult to explain."

"Like what kind of difficult things?" Fili asked. He looked lost.

"I don't know," Hector said. "Mysteries." Papá and Fili waited for him to say more. Hector tried to think of an easier example, but the only other mythological figure that came to mind was the Minotaur and he had no idea what mystery a man with a head of a bull represented. It was his father who finally came to his aid.

"I think I know what you mean, Hector. When I was galloping on Cometa, going as fast as the wind, I felt like the horse and me were one. Her legs were like my legs and her power was my power and she went wherever I wanted her to go. All I had to do was think about going one way, and that's where Cometa went. We were one. She was my legs and I was her head. I was one of those centaurs. I was a centaur."

"But . . ." Fili said, "those centaurs were real, right? They had to be. How could anyone make them up if they hadn't seen them?"

"They're real, all right," Hector's father insisted. "That's what I'm trying to tell you."

"Yeah," Fili said. "I think they are. I'd like to be one of them centaurs."

"I give up," Hector said, standing up. "You two are hopeless."

He couldn't keep himself from laughing along with his father and Fili as he stepped out of the bedroom.

"Wait, Hector, wait!" Hector's father called. Hector stopped, turned to face his father. "I want to tell you something." Hector waited. There was sadness in his father's voice. "These centaurs are real. They're good to know. They're not confused like most of us. They aren't men that act like horses, or horses that want to be men. They know who they are. They're happy to be centaurs. They have the best of both worlds, the brain of a man and the heart of a horse. They're balanced. Not like us. We're wild horses when we should be thinking, and thinking when we should be galloping with the heart of a wild horse. It's so hard to be both at the same time."

"Okay," Hector said. He waited for his father to explain the meaning behind his words. But his father only looked at him with eyes that were dimming. Hector nodded, as if he understood, although he didn't, and then walked out of the room.

Now, lying in his top bunk, Hector remembered his father's words. *They're balanced.* His father had used those exact words when referring to the centaurs, Hector was sure. In the dream at the hospital when Hector asked his father to take him, his father had responded: *It's not balanced yet.* Hector had assumed that the *it* in *it's not balanced* was the fact that Joey was alive and Fili was dead. But what if the *it* was what Hector needed—the balance of a centaur? Fat chance of that ever happening. He was no Fili, no matter how much his father wanted him to be. There was no balance in him. He was all cowardice and hate.

"Hey, Clinto! You awake?" It was Sansón speaking from the bottom bunk. He had been discharged from the infirmary the day before.

"No."

"You nervous about the fight?"

"What fight?"

"Mr. Díaz teach you some things?"

"Yeah."

"He boxed in prison, you know?"

"He sounded like he knew what he was talking about."

"A round is only two minutes, so that's all you need to do. Stay on your feet. One round. Two minutes. People are betting you won't make it one round."

"That's good to know. Thank you for telling me that."

"You all right? You sound different."

"No, man. I was just remembering something I haven't thought of in a long time. It caught me by surprise."

"It's Mr. Díaz's flashlight. It happens to me too. What you see?"

"Nothing. Do you really think Topo and I are hooked to each other like the old man and the fish?"

"Maybe *you're* hooked. I don't see that kid caring about you one way or another. He was just assigned to be the chief handler for one of the puppies. That's huge, ese. It's like the best job at Furman. It gets you out of all other work details including kitchen and toilets. How he got that job ahead of all the kids that wanted it? No sé. Could be that Colonel Taylor's rewarding him for signing on. That's the only explanation I can think of. That and the dog loves him like his own mama."

"Signing on?"

"To Furman. As when a kid *wants* to be here."

"Damn," Hector said softly to himself. The same person who'd caved his brother's skull was the chief handler of a puppy. Here he was sacrificing everything for revenge, and Joey's out there pursuing happiness. He had to admit that Joey seemed different after the septic tank. More serious and focused. Sansón was right; Joey couldn't care less about him. It wasn't as if Joey was ignoring him. It was if Hector had disappeared from the ambit of Joey's brain.

Hector heard Sansón's snores a few minutes later. He knew that there would be no sleep for him that night. He'd be lucky to keep his eyes open by the time the fight took place. The fight. Was it possible to stop hating Joey? It was not possible. It was impossible. The more Joey moved on to happier things, the greater the voltage of Hector's rage. Furman got Joey to sign on to some kind of future. Joey the drug addict, killer, evil being. There was no way he would let Joey pursue happiness. What he needed was a way to mess up Joey's mind. He needed to dominate him mentally. Joey had to have some secret he guarded, something he feared. A place in his past where he was vulnerable. It dawned on Hector that he knew where to find just what he needed.

Hector slid carefully out of his bunk. He got dressed and then he walked to Antonini's room. He reached in and got the alarm key just like he had planned. Once outside, he moved slowly but with purpose. There were spotlights on the entrance and sides of the dorms and on the perimeter of the property, but he still had the sense that he was invisible. Hector imagined what he would do with the information he found. Maybe whisper some of it in Joey's ear during the fight or maybe shout it out loud for all to hear. He would find a way to finally humiliate him, as he had been humiliated.

He climbed into Dr. Luna's office through the same window he had peered through before. He closed the curtains when he was inside and then turned on the lamp on Dr. Luna's desk. He noticed a computer terminal. Hopefully, Dr. Luna did not keep Joey's file digitally. He found the small key under the bronze eagle and opened the middle drawer of the cabinet where he thought the "M" files would be. The files in the middle drawer ended with Lopez. It was in the bottom drawer that Hector found the file for José Mendez.

On the left side of the file there were Dr. Luna's handwritten notes. The handwriting was almost impossible to read. Hector deciphered a few words: *addictive, progress, adapting, positive emotional response, social integration*. Hector stopped reading. He got the message. Joey and Furman were getting along fabulously. On the right side of the file was a more formal report from a Dr. James Casas, PhD. There was a short introduction by Dr. Casas. He had interviewed José Mendez on various occasions at the request of the Juvenile Probation Department and Judge Lisa Galvan. After that Hector read:

At age thirteen, José Mendez (the Juvenile) witnessed the murder of his mother, Merlinda Chavez Mendez, by his father, Horacio Clavel Mendez. Father turned the gun on himself and committed suicide immediately after killing his wife, also in the presence of the Juvenile. A subsequent medical examination of the Juvenile revealed signs of repeated physical abuse, most likely by the deceased father. Since then, the Juvenile has been living with his stepbrother (the deceased father's son by a previous marriage), Ignacio Mendez. The Texas Department of Family and Protective Services determined that the Juvenile's welfare was best served by living with his stepbrother, Ignacio, who was twenty-one at the time. This decision was made despite indications (from conversations that the mother had with a neighbor) that the Juvenile had been sexually abused during childhood. Protective Services determined without any further investigation that the perpetrator of the sexual abuse was the deceased father. My professional opinion, however, based on extensive interviews with the Juvenile, is that the perpetrator(s) was likely both the Juvenile's father as well as the stepbrother. The abuse seemed to have stopped when the Juvenile was ten years old, but it is clear that there remain ambivalent feelings in the Juvenile toward his stepbrother (he fears him but is dependent on him for his survival). This has resulted in the Juvenile turning to opiate use for mitigation of long-held trauma—

Hector slammed the file shut. He couldn't read any more. There was a part of him that was happy that Joey's life had been unimaginably wretched. He deserved it and should get more of the same or worse. And there was another part that felt disgusted at himself for the pleasure he was taking in another human being's suffering. His mind was splitting, destroying itself with conflict. Hate and something else, something tender and fragile and weak, were going at it bare-fisted in the boxing ring inside his head. The two energies could not live together anymore. It was a brotherhood gone berserk. They were fighting for supremacy. It was a duel to the death. Which force was the stronger of the two?

Hector went outside and threw himself on the ground. He grabbed on to tufts of grass to keep from falling backward into the black universe. He banged his forehead against the earth with all the strength in his body. He should have been the one who died, not Fili. Maybe it wasn't too late to join Fili. Would his father even take him if he killed himself? Joey was a chief dog handler! Damn, abused Joey was pursuing happiness full speed ahead. The sorry bastard had found a home. Was Hector supposed to feel happy for him? Sorry for what his father and his stepbrother had done to him? Damn pitiful piece of crap. He should have let him drown in mierda.

Hector turned on his back. He removed a small rock from his forehead and felt the bruise it had made there. What the hell was happening to him? He might as well just stay there and wait for Dr. Luna to find him next Sunday. Ever since he'd gotten to Furman, people had been giving him advice about hatred and cowardice, and their words had simply bounced off some invisible shield that surrounded him. Nothing penetrated the radiation emitted by hate. *Who are you afraid to disappoint?* Sansón had asked him. *Give up on revenge*, Cortina had advised. But here he was not willing to let go of his hatred for Joey, even after what he learned about his miserable life, even after he saved the kid's ass. He needed hate. Now more than ever. Hate was keeping him from something that seemed even worse than prison. Díaz said he had a certain kind of courage. It was hatred that gave him this courage. Even when he'd saved Joey, he'd acted out of hate. Hate would not be satisfied by letting Joey die that way. Hatred demanded to be fed with violence. That's the only kind of courage he had—the courage of hate.

And this courage was what he would show Joey in the ring.

CHAPTER 23

The boxing gloves were big, black, and soft. They reminded Hector of burned marshmallows.

"They're sixteen ounces, but they do the trick," X-Man said as he fastened the Velcro strap around the left-hand glove. "I've seen kids get knocked out cold with these."

Hector stood in one of the corners of a square constructed by rope tied to four metal chairs. The "boxing ring" was in the back of Yoda's toolshed. It looked like the whole Furman student body had shown up for the event. Antonini, who was to referee the fight, was fastening the gloves on Joey. Hector observed Joey. In a way, it was good to see that old killer stare coming from him. Hector could feel fear coming into him, just like back there at the Piggly Wiggly parking lot. For once, Hector welcomed the fear.

"The colonel got gloves with Velcro so when two kids needed to go at it, they could put the gloves on by themselves." X-Man looked around at the gathering crowd. "Listen, most of the betting is on whether you'll be standing after one round. No one's betting you'll win the fight. So, the objective here is to—"

"One round, I know. Before you go—help me take off my T-shirt."

"What the hell is that?" X-Man asked when Hector's shirt came off.

"It stands for courage," Hector told him.

"You people are strange," X-Man said before stepping out of the ring.

Hector danced in his corner and swung his arms around, windmill-style. He looked for Sansón, but the big guy was not there. It seemed like a year or two had passed since the day he'd asked X-Man to set up a grudge match with Joey. Why had he been so interested in fighting Joey? To show Joey he no longer feared him. To hit Joey in the face with all his pent-up rage—for the pleasure that would bring. He wanted to transform himself in such a way that Joey would fear him. That was not likely to happen. Nothing that Hector could do to Joey could be worse than what his father and stepbrother had already done to him. So, the objective now was what? To make sure Joey did not forget Fili. Let the kid remember that he was hated. And maybe sometime during the fight Hector would find a way to grind the kid's mental toughness into the ground.

Antonini motioned for Hector to come to the middle of the

ring. Joey and Hector faced each other. Joey grinned when he saw the C. Hector expected an insult or at least a smirk, but the look on Joey's face contained a tinge of admiration, like an artist proud of his work.

"We'll go three two-minute rounds. The rounds start and end when I blow the whistle. No wrestling. No throwing people to the ground. No kicking. No hitting the nuts of your opponent. If the other guy falls down, you go to your corner until I tell you. If you want the fight to stop, all you need to do is look at me and nod. Bump gloves."

Joey stretched his right arm out, and Hector reluctantly touched the glove at the end of it.

X-Man was back in Hector's corner with a bottle of water. Antonini came over and said to X-Man, "Ten on your kid making it one round."

"The ref can bet?" Hector asked.

"Yeah, man. That's good. Antonini has a good eye. He bets on the fighter he thinks is hungrier."

Hector remembered the words in Azi's note. *The Lord is the strength of my life, of whom shall I be afraid?* He was trying to remember the psalm number when he heard Antonini's whistle.

When he turned around, Joey was already in the middle of the ring, coming at him. Hector had one brief moment to remember Díaz's advice about moving and jabbing when he felt something like a brick hit his face. What he saw were not stars like all the books said. He saw tiny pinpricks of orange light blinking on and off. When he came to, he was on his knees struggling to get up. He heard cheers in the far-off distance.

"You want me to stop this?" Antonini asked, kneeling in front of him.

"Do you have to?"

"No."

Hector stood and squinted until the two images of Joey merged into one. There was something he wanted to tell Joey. It was on the tip of his consciousness. What was it? Joey had a stepladder. No, not a ladder . . . but a step something. It was easier to hate than to mourn. Someone told him that once. Maybe Mr. Lozano. But why would Mr. Lozano say that to him? Maybe because Mr. Lozano lost his son in Iraq. Hector was running backward, being chased by a slobbering pit bull. No wonder the dogs loved Joey. He was one of them. Joey launched another ferocious right hand. Hector felt a swish of air pass by his lips. Stepbrother. The word crystallized at the very moment that Joey's glove found Hector's left ear. Hector managed to stay on his feet, but he was tottering sideways, looking for something to grab. He felt a warm liquid ooze out into his ear canal. It felt good, like pool water finally coming out. He raised both hands to his face as Joey pummeled the top of his arms, shoulders, ribs. Behind his gloves, Hector could see Joey's face. He wanted to kill. You had to hand it to Joey. He could be evil when he wanted to be, no regrets. Joey was not divided like he was, struggling with the fear of going to prison, or of disappointing his mother and Aurora. Joey would have watched Hector sink in the septic tank, no problem. You had to admire Joey for his simplicity.

And for his strength. Even with his hands on his face, Hector could feel the power behind Joey's punches. The punches that hurt the most were the ones to Hector's abdomen. But what good were punches down there? It was the hurt inside his head that needed putting out. Hector lowered his gloves, invited Joey to hit him.

Time passed. Seconds? Hours? Days? Hector heard kids shout, "Stay down! Stay down! Get up! Get up!" and had no idea why they were shouting that until he saw Antonini's face hovering above him and Hector realized he was sprawled on the grass. His legs were probably akimbo. He had always liked that word.

"What time is it?" Hector asked.

Antonini laughed. "There's a minute left in the round. Is that what you're asking?"

Hector turned on his side. He heard some cheers and some boos. "Did he hit me?"

"One of the best right hooks I've seen," Antonini said. "Stay down."

Hector spat. He tasted blood. He knelt on one knee and then slowly made his way up. Antonini turned him around so he could face Joey. Joey rushed at him. He was both frustrated and determined. Hector watched him approach. He waited for Joey to get close, and then his right hand exploded on the tip of Joey's nose. Joey's head barely moved back with the impact, but immediately blood started streaming out of both nostrils. It wasn't a trickle. It was a deluge. Joey stood there stunned, using his tongue to keep the blood from entering his mouth. He looked at Hector in a new way, as if unable to believe that Hector would actually hit him. Before Joey could recover, Hector unloaded another jab on Joey's lips. This woke Joey up. Hector saw that the power and force that Joey had used up to then was only a fraction of what Joey possessed. Now all that Hector could do was move around the square trying to evade the hurricane of punches thrown at him. There it was—real, burning-hot rage. Good, honest, undiluted hatred was pouring out of Joey. When Joey finally got close to him, Hector wrapped his arms around Joey's shoulders, restraining his arms. Hector felt the blood from Joey's nose on his chest and then felt it dribble down over the C that Joey had carved. Hector thought of saying the truth about

Joey's father, about his stepbrother, about both of them. But something stopped him from uttering the words. Not fear and certainly not kindness, but memories: Fili's arms wrapped around him, carrying him out of the Lions banquet. Fili at Pepe's, blushing when Hector asked if he loved Gloria. Fili explaining how he planned to pay for the house in Socorro. The memories came, wrapped in sorrow and joy, as if liberated by Joey's punches. It's easier to hate than to mourn. It was Cortina who'd told him that. Now Hector understood. What he whispered to Joey was this: "You don't scare me anymore."

Joey tried to pull himself out of Hector's grasp, but Hector wouldn't let him. The whistle finally blew. Hector had never imagined that 120 seconds could last so long. He let Joey out of the bear hug. The look on Joey's face was far from friendly, but it wasn't hatred either.

Antonini and X-Man worked on Joey's nose during the break, but there was no stopping the blood. After about five minutes of pinching and sticking cotton swabs up Joey's nostrils with no success, Antonini waved his hands to signify that the fight was over. There was hardly any reaction from the crowd. The betting had been on his ability to make it through one round, and a handful of students were collecting money from the rest of the crowd.

Hector watched Joey and Antonini walk off toward the

infirmary. His wish of hitting Joey had come through, and he felt sad and disappointed as he watched them go. He still hated Joey. He still felt like a coward. Kids were coming over and congratulating him—not so much, he gathered, for the two lucky punches that he threw, but for getting up after being knocked out. He should be proud of himself for winning the fight, but he felt empty and lonely. He wished he was alone. He wanted to be with the memories of Fili that were starting to come. He didn't want them to go away.

"We struck the mother lode!" X-Man waved a handful of bills in Hector's face. "Two hundred and twenty buckaroos! We cleaned up on those who bet you wouldn't make it through one round and on those who bet on Joey to win the whole thing."

"That's your money," Hector said.

"You know, I can get Rosa in the kitchen to buy some steaks for us. She'll cook them for us too." X-Man was untying the rope from the chairs.

"No thanks."

"We lucked out, Clinto. That kid's nostrils were like dry leaves from all the dope he's smoked."

"Yeah. We lucked out."

"But you kept getting up. You earned some respect."

Respect. The word sickened him. Fili would be alive if Chavo had not craved respect after Gloria broke up with him.

Respect and disrespect. Killing and revenge and cowardice. Stupid, meaningless words, all of them. None of them worth dying for.

In the distance, Hector saw the backhoe Yoda used to dig out the septic tank. There was a tree by the septic tank that threw good shade. It seemed like a good place to sit for a while. Hector took his shirt from X-Man's hand.

"Thanks for setting up the grudge match," he said.

Then he walked in the direction of the tree. He sat under its shade and hugged his knees. The sorrow of Fili's loss was there waiting for him. Hector didn't turn away from it. It came in powerful waves at first, and then it became a river that carried other painful stuff: guilt, shame, hatred, arrogance, jealousy. Hector let it flow. Watched all of it. It was all part of him.

When the sun started to go down, Hector stood and said to Fili, "I miss you. It's not balanced yet, I know. I'll do what I can to make it right. I will."

CHAPTER 24

That evening, after Sansón was asleep, Hector turned on his desk and read Azi's email. He had postponed reading because he thought that it would make him feel things he didn't want to feel. But now there was nothing to lose. He was going to complete his mission at Furman that night, and it didn't matter what he felt.

Hello Hector,

Aurora mentioned that you got an hour of internet a week, so I hope this finds its way to you. First, your mother and Aurora are doing well. They are grieving for Fili and they miss you, but they are carrying on. My mom and your mom have become best friends, and I enjoy spending as much time as I can with Aurora. She makes me laugh, and that's good a thing for me and for her.

I don't want you to feel bad about not talking to me the last days you were here. I really understand. I'm taking it as a sign of how much our friendship means to you—that seeing me made it harder for you to leave.

I've been thinking a lot lately about our essays on the pursuit of happiness. I don't know why I find it comforting to think that we both wrote about what the pursuit of happiness meant to our fathers. I like how both our fathers found happiness in living for others. Your father went from picking fruit to making pants in a factory to working as an auto mechanic. He fulfilled his duty to provide for his family, but he also eventually found a job that he loved. And I know for a fact that my father found happiness in doing God's work. My favorite line in your essay is this one: "Happiness is what you like to do, and duty is what you need to do. But what if the duty comes from love?"

Remember when you were in the hospital and you told me you were a coward? I couldn't understand how wanting to stay alive was cowardice. But now I see the many ways we can live as cowards, like when we run from the duty that comes from love. It takes so much courage, Hector, to pursue happiness, like our fathers did.

I'm sorry to get so serious here. I'm not sure when I will hear from you, and I wanted to say all this to you.

I pray that it will help you. Will you write to us? To your mother, to Aurora, and to me. I'm including myself in the group of people who need you and are waiting for your return.

Azi

Hector pushed his chair back as quietly as possible and stood. He looked out the window and saw night lit by the full moon. He turned off the lamp on his desk. He looked at the sleeping Sansón one last time and then walked out and opened the door to Antonini's room. The door screeched. He stopped. He felt his heart pick up the tempo of its beat. His mouth was dry. He pushed the door open just enough for his body to fit through. A sound came from the back where Antonini slept. He waited. When the silence returned, he stepped into the room and lifted the alarm key.

Out in the hall, he inserted the key into the black box and turned it. The red light turned to green. He opened the steel doors to dorm D and stepped out into the night. He looked up and saw a questioning expression on the face of the full moon. *What are you doooing, Hector?* But he was tired of trying to answer questions, so he went out into the night imagining that he was on Cometa, the horse his father loved so much. His father's words came to him. *Sometimes we think when we should be galloping with the heart of a wild horse.* That was it. He was galloping even if each step was slow and deliberate. There was something liberating about the sight of a million stars. Any moment his feet would lift off the ground and he would be pulled up into the vastness of the universe. His heart was beating harder and faster now, but amazingly there was no fear. No fear. How long had he waited to feel that?

The toolshed was open. Yoda never locked the doors. A kid could come in there and get an ax or a chain saw or any number of murderous tools anytime he wanted. All Hector needed was the hammer. Hector left the door to the toolshed open, and with the light from the full moon, he saw it there, hanging quietly on a pegboard. It was an old hammer that had seen a lot of use. Its wood handle was smooth, and its steel head was perfectly balanced. It was molded with time and use to fit in Hector's hand.

Hector noticed the tremor in his hand as he inserted the key into the alarm box of dorm C. It was the normal rush of adrenaline. The body acting out the fight-or-flight instincts even if the mind was . . . what? Committed. That word always made Hector smile. He finally got his hand steady enough to turn off the alarm. He went in, looked for room C-18. If dorm C was numbered the same way as dorm D, then C-18 would be the fourth room on the right, on the first floor.

Hector pulled the chair from the desk and sat in front of the bed. There was Joey on his side curled up like a baby. There was a strong odor of perspiration coming from his body. The Furman habits of good hygiene had not yet rubbed off on Joey. Joey's eyes twitched behind his eyelids. Joey moaned, "No, no." Some past terror was playing out inside his head.

Hector closed his eyes and remembered the face that Joey had made when he walked in front of the truck. The expression of contempt when he saw Hector safely in the cabin. Now Hector felt an electricity on his arms, as if his body wanted to make sure that he did not freeze again, like he did back when his hand froze on the handle of the truck, when he could not move to open the door. The hammer lay on his lap. Hector hit the palm of his left hand with it. All body parts were loose and in working order. There was Joey's temple not two feet away from him. It was a soft part of the head. What would Joey feel? What did Fili feel? An explosion of white or of black and then nothing. Now was the time to right the balance.

"Hey," Hector whispered. "Wake up."

Joey opened his eyes. First there was shock and then relief. It wasn't some ghost or the devil, only Hector. "What you doing here?" Joey asked sleepily. Then, noticing the hammer in Hector's hand, "Man, you gotta be kiddin' me."

"Does it look like I'm kidding?"

Joey sat up, leaned back against the bed. He rubbed his eyes. There was a bloody cotton ball stuck in one of Joey's nostrils. "Coulda done it while I was sleeping."

"Yeah, I could have. But I wanted you to see me."

Joey looked at Hector. "All right, I saw you. What now?" Hector had to hand it to Joey. The kid was fearless. Or maybe Hector was simply incapable of inciting fear in him.

"I have to do something," Hector said.

"Shhh, you'll wake up the RA."

But Hector knew that Joey wasn't so fearless after all. He was afraid of getting kicked out of Furman. He was afraid of returning to the projects and his stepbrother. "You like this place," Hector said, as if pointing out a weakness in Joey's character.

Joey didn't answer. He lowered his eyes, embarrassed, and that was answer enough for Hector.

Someone down the hall coughed. Joey said, "How you get through the alarm?"

Hector dangled the key hanging from his neck. Joey made a face like he was impressed.

There was a long silence. Hector noticed perspiration on Joey's forehead. He saw Joey's Adam's apple move up and down nervously. The fight-or-flight energy had kicked up inside of Joey as well. Hector asked, "That day at the Piggly Wiggly, did you mean what you said about killing me?"

Joey narrowed his eyebrows for a moment, deep in thought. "I wanted to see you squirm."

"Why?"

"You were an asshole."

Hector thought about it. It was possible that Joey was right. But if he was an asshole then, what was he now? "Were you going to kill me or not?" The question seemed to have some bearing on the present situation, but Hector wasn't clear how.

"I don't know. Maybe. You were starting to piss me off again." Joey kept his eyes on Hector's hand holding the hammer. He was playing it cool, but he was ready to react. Joey licked his lips, said tentatively, "Your brother disrespected my brother."

You mean your stepbrother, Hector thought of saying but didn't. "Gloria had already broken up with Chavo when my brother started dating her."

"Your brother shoulda talked to Chavo first. That would show respect."

"My brother showed respect when he tried to talk to Chavo in the church parking lot. Your . . . brother was an asshole and you know it." Hector and Joey locked eyes. There was a momentary look of fear in Joey's eyes. "It didn't seem like your brother was interested in listening. You didn't seem to be interested in talking either when you swung that bat."

"It happened like I told that judge! It was fast. I thought

Fili was strangling Chavo." Joey's words started out loud and immediately softened to a whisper. His words almost sounded like an apology.

There was nothing more for Hector to say about the afternoon at the church parking lot. He hadn't come to get any apologies from Joey. He cleared his throat and spoke, looking directly at Joey. "We have a situation here. Probably best if we went outside."

"You wanna try to kill me with that hammer? Inside or outside we're gonna end up making noise. Get both of us kicked out of here."

"You can tell the colonel I started it. I came to you."

"It won't work. I fight back even to defend myself, I'm out. The colonel told me when we got here." Joey swiped the top of his head with his hand, then rubbed the sweat off. "You don't even know what you doin'. Don't be stupid!"

Joey's words reminded Hector of Aurora. Not so much because Aurora also called him stupid on occasion, but because of Joey's tone. As if Joey were the smart one now, telling him not to be stupid. It was strange to hear Joey, of all people, watching out for his future. There was something different about the Joey sitting there in front of him from the Joey who carved the C on his chest. There was a light in his eyes that was not there before. *Joey's pursuit of happiness*, Hector thought. "Inside or outside. It's up to you." Hector returned Joey's stare with all the strength he had accumulated since that afternoon at the church parking lot. He saw in Joey's face the recognition of that strength. Joey kicked the sheet from his body and swung his legs to the floor. "Can I put my pants on?"

Outside the steel doors of dorm C there were three concrete steps. Hector sat on the top step and waited for Joey to do the same. Joey lowered himself slowly, cautiously.

"Put your hand out." Hector tapped the space between them with the hammer.

"What?"

"It's the only way I can think of."

"Only way for what?"

"For making things balanced."

"What you talkin' about? You wanna smash my hand?" Joey asked, incredulous. "You crazy?"

"You left a mark on me." Hector lifted his T-shirt and turned so Joey could see his chest. "I leave a mark on you. It will be a bigger mark because you also killed my brother. I only temporarily crippled yours. It's not completely balanced, but it's better than what we have now."

Joey laughed. Shook his head. Stuck his hands under his thighs. "Estás loco."

"Put your hand out!"

"Or what?"

"We fight. There'll be enough noise to wake people up. We'll be gone from Furman. I don't care, but you seem to."

"Maybe I just kill you. Bury you out by that septic tank."

"The one where I saved your ass?"

Hector could see a flicker of gratitude come over Joey's face. Then his mental wheels started turning again. "People will see me with a busted hand. They'll know something's up."

"I'll do one finger. You can pick which one. You can say it got caught in those doors." Hector pointed at the steel doors behind him. "Tell them you were sleeping on the top bunk and you rolled off. Landed on your finger."

Joey grunted.

"Listen, man. This is the only way I can think of to stop the pain in my head. I either get on with life, like you're doing, or go to prison or get killed by you. Those are my only options. We do this. It's over for me. I'm square with my brother. It's over. No more revenge. You can kill me later if you still want to."

Joey swore under his breath. Then, turning to Hector, hissing with old hatred, "I *will* kill you. This time for sure."

"I know it."

Joey moved farther away from Hector, placed his right

hand on the concrete, fingers spread. Then, "Wait. That's my shooting hand." It took Hector a moment to realize that Joey was talking basketball. Joey stood and moved to the right of Hector. Just as Joey sat down, Hector stood up again and walked a few feet, looked on the ground, came back with a stick.

"Which finger?" Hector spread Joey's hand.

"Not the middle one. I need that one for every time I see you."

"The small one."

Joey nodded. He put the stick in his mouth and bit it. Then he shut his eyes.

Hector took a deep breath. He thought of Fili, spoke to him. *It won't be fully balanced. But it's something. I hope you understand.* He opened his eyes. Raised the hammer over his head, held it there for a moment, and then he brought the head of the hammer with all his force, with all his rage.

Joey jumped up. His face was contorted with pain. He held his hand in his armpit, his teeth still clamped on the stick. He went off to the side of the dorms, sat on the ground. Hector stood over him for a moment and then sat next to him. After a while, Joey extended his hand. The finger already looked like a miniature eggplant. "It'll heal," Hector said. "But it will stay crooked. Now you got something to remember me. Like I got something to remember you."

"Get out . . . of my face." Joey wiped the wetness in his cheek with the forearm of his good hand.

"You have to go back inside so I can turn the alarm back on." Hector stood first and waited for Joey. When they were standing, Hector took off his shirt and grabbed Joey's arm. Joey shook it off.

"I don't want your stinking shirt!"

"Then wrap the hand with one of yours when you get in. Soak it in cold water. Morning call is only about an hour away. Someone will take you to the hospital. It looks broken."

In front of the doors, just before stepping in, Joey said, glancing quickly at Hector, "You still the same coward you ever was."

"I know it. I can live with that."

When Joey was inside, Hector turned the alarm back on. The moon was hidden behind dark clouds. The stars were disappearing, and the night was turning dark blue. Hector cleaned the hammer and returned to Yoda's shop. It was almost over, but there was still something he needed to do.

He walked to Dr. Luna's office, opened the window, and climbed in. He turned on the computer on the desk and waited. It did not require a password. He took that as a signal from his brother and father in heaven that they approved of his actions. He clicked on his email account and wrote two emails. The first one was to his mother via Aurora.

Mami,

I'm sorry I haven't written. I will write more soon, I promise. I'm okay. This place is just like a regular school. The only bad part about it is that it's so far from you. I miss you and Aurora, and I miss Fili. But, Mami, it's really important that we carry through with his plan to move to Socorro. That's what he would want and what Papá would want as well. I want that too, Mami, for us and for me. It will help me to know I will be living in that beautiful house with you and Aurora when I get out.

Tu hijo que te quiere mucho,

Hector

The second email was to Azi.

Azi,

I don't know how to describe all that's been happening inside of me. It's like a game of chess inside my head—with two kings and their armies fighting for control. I'm not sure the right king is going to win. It looks like the match is headed for a draw right now. But a draw is good. A draw will still allow me to pursue happiness, the way our fathers pursued it. You're right, it will take courage. But I got people helping me. Here at Furman and also when I get back home. It's hard to believe that you have stuck with me despite all you've seen in me. I see now that Fili's death, and my father's, are wounds that need to heal. It may take a while. I'm just barely beginning to feel the pain that comes from them. I'm hoping you'll be with me as I go through this. I could sure use someone lots smarter than me.

How do you say *thank you* in Farsi?

Hector

Hector cleared the entry into his email account from the computer's browser history before shutting it off. He jumped out the window and then stretched out on the ground. It was the same spot where he had once tried to keep himself from falling into the darkness of the universe. Now he lay on his back, exhausted. He looked at a cluster of stars and thought that they looked like the constellation of Sagittarius. He could kind of make out the bow and the arrow. Maybe. That would be something—to see a centaur up there on this particular night.

CHAPTER 25

Hector was mowing the entrance to Furman Academy. He was lucky to get the assignment. Everyone wanted to ride the new John Deere 5510 with a mower attached. The thing was sleek. Yoda showed him how to drive, and Hector surprised himself by how well he could handle it. There was no gear shifting involved, true, but the machine still required a certain hand-eye-brain coordination to go around trees and boulders and to mow as close as possible to the edge of sidewalks without busting the blades. But it was the combination of monotony and movement that Hector liked the most. His mind could float here and there unfettered on the long stretches of grass and then zero in on the task at hand when concentration was required.

The afternoon sun was bright, and Hector pulled down the visor of his blue Furman cap. He would have borrowed X-Man's aviator sunglasses except that X-Man took them with him to a real outside detail. X-Man and six other lucky students were loaned out to paint a halfway home for girls. Heaven descended upon Furman now and then. It was indoor work, but X-Man said the dark glasses were to women what pollen was to bees.

In the distance, Hector could see Interstate 10 congested with commuters going home. And what was to stop him from pointing the tractor west and heading to El Paso? Without the mower dragging behind him, he could probably make the tractor go twenty miles an hour, maybe more. He'd be there in a week or so. Hector saw himself pulling off the high-way at the Horizon Boulevard exit, then turning right on Alameda and on to the new house in Socorro. Aurora told him in her last email that Manny had painted the outside of the house "parrot green"—*It's so bright that if you stood on the moon and looked down, you could see it*, she wrote. Mami had immediately planted white, pink, and red roses so the whole yard looked like one of the dresses she used to wear in Mexico when Papá had been courting her.

Hector reached the edge of the front lawn and stopped. He calculated in his mind the time he had remaining at Furman. Technically, three more months, but Mr. Díaz told him he could write to Judge Galvan. Maybe he could go home next month, in time to start his junior year at Socorro High

School. Hector sighed and turned the tractor for another pass at the lawn. It should have been a no-brainer, but here he was, mulling it over. It's not that he didn't want to go home— he did. He wanted to see his mother and Aurora and Azi.

But if he went home next month, what would happen to the chess club that he'd started at Furman, which now had five members? And Sansón? They were halfway through *The Count of Monte Cristo,* and at the rate they were going, it would be another year or two before they finished. And who would be there to listen to Mr. Díaz go on and on about the mind's flashlight? Every time he thought about leaving Furman, Hector felt the double whammy of happiness and sadness.

And then there was Joey.

It was not exactly accurate to say that Hector would miss the kid. Still, there was a tension, an alertness, an aliveness that Joey brought to him. Joey was sticking around Furman until his eighteenth birthday, when he would join the army and train to be a Military Working Dog Handler. Judge Galvan had already signed off on the plan. All this information had come to Hector from X-Man . . . for a very small fee.

The animosity between Joey and Hector was still there. Joey threw Hector the finger whenever he saw him. It was just the little finger, but the message was clear. Now and then Hector would respond by lifting his T-shirt and flashing

Joey with the C on his chest. Joey's crooked finger reminded Hector of *The Old Man and the Sea*. It turned out that Sansón was right: Joey was the old man and Hector was the tuna on the hook.

Hector had managed to tear himself free, but the gash made by the hook would last forever.

AUTHOR'S NOTE

This book is a new novel, but it contains some bones from an earlier novel of mine. In 2007, a year or so after my first young adult novel, *Behind the Eyes*, came out, I visited a reformatory school in Minneapolis where the students were reading the book. On the way back home, I was filled with the sense that the book had not given the students all that it could have given them. The young men in the school had not fully seen themselves in Hector's fears and hopes and moral decisions. When, years later, the rights reverted to me, I decided to retell Hector's story in an entirely new way.

On the Hook is that new book. Some of the characters have kept their old names, but they are different people—more real, more complex, more dynamic. What happens to them and how they respond is also deeper and more intricate. My intention for the work is different. I wrote *Behind the Eyes* when my son and daughter were fifteen and thirteen and I wanted them to glimpse at what their father's life was like growing up in the projects of El Paso. Now my children are parents themselves and I would like my grandchildren and other young people to know about the courage of love in a world where hatred is so pervasive.

ACKNOWLEDGMENTS

I am grateful to my friends at Scholastic for their continuing faith in my work. Arthur A. Levine and Cheryl Klein always believed in the book's potential. Their wisdom and patience guided me as I searched for the novel's new vision. And I am especially grateful to Emily Seife and David Levithan, the editors of the final draft. Their brilliant work helped me bring out all the beauty and power in Hector's story. I am forever indebted to Faye Bender of The Book Group, who has been there for me since the beginning. I want to thank my young friends Cassandra Rios and Amelia Gaytan for their helpful comments on an early draft. Most of all, I want to offer this book to all the young people who find themselves in difficult places. May you find hope here.

ABOUT THE AUTHOR

Francisco X. Stork emigrated from Mexico at the age of nine with his mother and stepfather. He is the author of eight novels, including: *Marcelo in the Real World*, recipient of the Schneider Family Book Award, *The Last Summer of the Death Warriors*, which received the Amelia Elizabeth Walden Award, and *The Memory of Light*, recipient of the Tomás Rivera Award. His most recent novels are *Disappeared*, which received four starred reviews and was a Walter Dean Myers Award Honor Book, and its companion, *Illegal*. He lives near Boston with his family. Visit him at franciscostork.com.